EXTRAORDINARY ACCLAIM
FOR THE WORKS OF
CAMERON JUDD

"Judd does his usual exquisite job of character development. This book will restore your faith in westerns."
—*El Paso Herald Post* on *Jerusalem Camp*

"Gripping and entertaining."
—*Virginian Tennessean* on *The Overmountain Men*

"Judd writes a mean story."
—*Zane Grey's West*

"An impressive performance . . . a classically simple, fast-paced tale. Marks Judd as a keen observer of the human heart as well as a fine action writer."
—*Publishers Weekly* on *Timber Creek*

"Abundance of historical detail . . . a heartfelt attempt to glimpse the soul of an American hero. By any standard, Judd succeeds."
—*Booklist* on *Crockett of Tennessee*

St. Martin's Paperbacks Titles
by Cameron Judd

FIREFALL

BRAZOS

DEAD MAN'S GOLD

DEVIL WIRE

THE GLORY RIVER

TEXAS FREEDOM

SNOW SKY

CORRIGAN

TIMBER CREEK

RENEGADE LAWMEN

THE HANGING AT LEADVILLE

KENTON'S CHALLENGE

CAMERON JUDD

St. Martin's Paperbacks

KENTON'S CHALLENGE

Copyright © 2001 by Cameron Judd.

ISBN: 0-312-98123-6

Printed in the United States of America

St. Martin's Paperbacks edition / November 2001

St. Martin's Paperbacks are published by St. Martin's Press, 175 Fifth Avenue, New York, NY 10010.

10 9 8 7 6 5 4 3 2 1

In order to fulfill one of her life goals,
this book is dedicated to Lauren Burns.

KENTON'S CHALLENGE

CHAPTER

1

ST. LOUIS, MISSOURI

THE SUN SANK WESTWARD, A WARM AFTERNOON GIV-
ing way to a chill that hurried the footsteps of under-
protected pedestrians rushing homeward to supper
tables and firesides.

Among the wind-nipped horde, Alex Gunnison,
newly named associate publisher of *Gunnison's Illustrated American,* the nation's most popular general-
interest magazine, walked without a shiver. In the
warmth of the afternoon he had regretted the woolen
suit he had chosen in the cold of morning, but now
he was glad for it. Comfort removed the necessity of
hurrying to reach his home and begin an evening that
loomed before him like an empty wasteland. With his
wife off in Colorado, the house he usually couldn't
wait to reach held little appeal for him tonight.

So he trudged while others hurried, his hands deep
in his pockets and his hat turned low to deflect the
wind. His house was four blocks ahead, the dog

awaited feeding in its pen, and the two cats were no doubt in their usual evening spots in the big side window, watching for his arrival.

He stopped and sighed. Let the cats wait. Tonight he felt too melancholy to go home. He'd go to Barrigan's instead and eat a leisurely supper, read the newspaper, maybe drink a few extra cups of coffee over dessert. Better that than languishing at home.

Speeding his pace, he headed for the next corner, made a left turn, and walked to Barrigan's, a favorite restaurant. He was greeted warmly at the door and conveyed to his usual table. Comments were made about the absence of his wife. "She's visiting relations in Colorado," he replied, "and I anticipate her return within the week."

Gunnison, who had eaten lightly through the day, was hungry and ordered a dinner built around pork chops and gravy. He sipped coffee while he waited and stared at the empty chair across from him where Roxanne normally sat. He and his wife ate at Barrigan's frequently, and it didn't feel quite right to be here without her. Better here alone than home alone, though.

He'd just received his plate when he noticed a heavyset man of about sixty approaching him from across the room, wearing rumpled clothing and the vaguely uneasy expression of one about to intrude into another's privacy. Gunnison sighed inwardly, anticipating being forced to talk to this man while his food went cold and uneaten on his plate before him.

"Beg your pardon, sir," the man said in a soft tone,

"but aren't you Mr. Alexander Gunnison?"

Gunnison hadn't been called Alexander in years. "I'm Alex Gunnison, yes."

"I thought you were, sure as the world! A man changes when he puts his boyhood behind, but there's always something of the boy remaining to mark him. In your case, it's the eyes."

Gunnison smiled with his lips and frowned with his eyes. "I'm afraid I'm at a loss, sir. . . . I think you must know me, but I have to admit I don't know you."

The man did what Gunnison had hoped he wouldn't: he scooted back the empty chair at Gunnison's table for two and sat down heavily. With elbows on the table and a warm smile on his face, he said, "I wouldn't expect you to recollect me, Mr. Gunnison . . . or can I call you Alexander, like I used to?"

"I go by Alex now."

"Well, Alex, you'd not be expected to recall me, as I said, but I sure do remember you as a boy, running all around your father's house and nigh knocking me off the ladder more than once. Oh, how your father would scold you! 'Let the men work, and be off with you,' he'd say. But I'd always stick up for you. I've enjoyed the presence of lively children all my days, ever since I raised my own brood."

"So you worked at my father's house when I was just a little boy."

"That's right. . . . My name's Bill Garry. You might remember me, eh?"

"I'm sorry, but I admit I don't." Garry had reached across the table to shake Gunnison's hand, and Gunnison clasped the hand, noting how callused and dirty it was. He'd find an excuse to slip to the washroom in a moment and scrub his hand clean before he ate.

"I was a carpenter in them days, back before I took a spill and hurt my back so I couldn't work no more. You remember when your father had that office room added onto the side of your house?"

"Yes, I think I do."

"I built them shelves that covered the two walls." Garry said it with pride.

"Really! Well, you'll be glad to know they're still standing, with not a sag in them."

"Oh, of course. What I build, I build to last. And how is your father?"

"He's well. But moving into retirement. He's made me associate publisher of the magazine." Gunnison wondered why he was volunteering information; all he was doing was assuring that the conversation would go on that much longer.

"Oh, I know all about it. I'm a faithful reader of the *Illustrated American*. Have been for years. I was proud to read of your advancement."

"Thank you."

Garry's smile faded as he went on: "But I was sad indeed to read of Mr. Kenton's passing away."

Gunnison nodded. "Yes."

"What a tragedy! For such a talent to be lost in so sad a way . . . I've missed him ever since. There's no one whose work compares to Brady Kenton's, and so I've always said. You've come close, Alex, but as you know, there'll never be another Brady Kenton."

"He was a remarkable man."

"I can't name another artist who became more famous doing what Kenton did."

"Kenton wasn't an artist. He was an illustrator," Gunnison clarified, then felt petty for saying it.

"Whatever you call what he did, I liked it. So did all of America, and hats off to your father's magazine for bringing Kenton to us." The man sounded almost emotional. Gunnison had run across this kind of Kenton devotion before. It made him more jealous than he wanted to admit. "Hard to believe that Kenton's dead."

He's not, Gunnison said in his mind, because for now that was the only way he could say it.

"People see him around, you know," Garry said.

"I hardly see how that's possible," Gunnison said, smiling tightly.

"Oh, lots of folks don't believe he's dead. He was always sort of a trickster, you know."

If only you knew, Gunnison thought.

Garry continued, "My brother Cordell, for example, who swears, absolutely swears, that he saw Brady Kenton himself not a week ago, in Colorado. It was a little mining town—for the life of me I can't recall the name of it. Cordell got back from Colorado two days ago and told me about it this very morning."

"He must have seen someone who resembled Kenton, that's all," Gunnison said.

"Perhaps, but Cordell met Kenton once, back in Chicago, and says he knows for a fact this was none other than the man."

"And you believe him?"

"I'd like to. I don't want to believe Kenton is gone."

"I understand. But I can assure you, Kenton is no longer here." Gunnison's wording was carefully chosen. He did not like to lie and tried to avoid it.

"And all the more sorrow to us for it. Well, anyway, I'll hope Cordell is right, and you are wrong."

"So do I."

Garry hesitated noticeably, then became quite serious in manner. "I hope you don't think me foolish for saying this . . . but I think you should investigate the possibility that Cordell *is* right. He was very sure he'd seen the authentic item in Colorado. Very sure."

Now there was no alternative but an outright lie. "I was there when he died, Mr. Garry. I saw his body. I'm afraid your brother can't possibly be right."

"All I can say is, he was mighty certain about it." Garry at last stood. "Well, I'll leave you to your meal. Sorry to have interrupted you."

"Not at all."

"Give my best to your father. Ask if he remembers me."

"I'll do that, Mr. Garry."

CHAPTER

2

GUNNISON STARED AT HIS PLATE A MOMENT BEFORE he began to eat. What Garry had just told him had unsettled him even though he had not let it show.

Kenton seen in Denver. Garry was the third person in just under two weeks to report such a sighting to Gunnison. The first two reports Gunnison had discounted, the second less easily than the first. But now a third. . . . What was he to think?

Gunnison picked up his fork and knife and sliced off a bite of pork. He ate but tasted it only slightly, his mind preoccupied.

It was possible Kenton was in fact in Colorado, at least theoretically. The news of Kenton's death, reported as fact in the *Illustrated American* and picked up subsequently by every major newspaper in the nation, was a fabrication, a fact known by only a handful of people, Gunnison chief among them. It was he who had written Kenton's obituary and who had eulogized his old partner movingly, standing beside a mahogany coffin weighted with old copies of the *Illustrated American.*

Gunnison still wondered if that deception, once revealed to the world, would cost him his position at the *Illustrated American,* a position greatly advanced since Kenton's supposed death. With Kenton thought to be gone forever, Gunnison's father, founder and publisher of the magazine, had at last advanced his son upward in rank, aiming him ultimately for the publisher's office. But once it was learned that Gunnison had cooperated with Kenton in foisting one of the greatest hoaxes in journalistic history upon the world—using the sacred *Illustrated American* to do it—Gunnison feared his own father would fire him. The senior Gunnison took his magazine and his conceptions of journalistic duty dead seriously. He would not abide deliberate deception, not from his own son, not from Brady Kenton, not from anyone.

It didn't matter. Gunnison would have carried out the hoax at almost any price, because Brady Kenton had asked him to. By becoming "dead" in the eyes of the world, Kenton had gained the opportunity to travel to England to seek his lost wife, Victoria, who for many years had been in the hands of the obsessed Dr. David Kevington. Kenton had taken with him his daughter, Rachel Frye.

But that had been nearly a year ago. Gunnison had received a single item of news from Kenton at the beginning, a letter sent to him at the *Illustrated American* office under a preagreed code name. The letter informed him that Kenton and Rachel had safely made their voyage and were preparing to begin the journey to the Kevington estate. Kenton promised another letter would soon follow . . . but none had ever come.

Gunnison had waited, waited, and waited more . . . but nothing.

He was worried. What if Kenton and Rachel had been captured by Kevington, or worse? The man had demonstrated his willingness to do extreme actions long ago when he'd taken the badly injured Victoria Kenton away from a train accident and spirited her off to his English estate. There he had slowly led her back to health again, though not before she had given birth to the daughter of Brady Kenton, conceived shortly before her accident. Victoria had never known of the birth; she was in a coma when Rachel Kenton was born and still in a coma when Rachel was given away to a servant family named Frye, to raise as their own.

Rachel had learned the secret of her true heritage many years later and had come to the United States and found Brady Kenton, her real father.

Now Kenton and Rachel were gone off to England . . . or perhaps off the face of the earth, for all Gunnison knew.

He worried almost constantly about the lack of news from Kenton and already was secretly planning a voyage of his own to England to find out what had happened to his friend.

But what if Kenton wasn't in England at all? Could he really be in Colorado?

If so, why hadn't he contacted Gunnison? And where were Rachel and Victoria?

Gunnison stared at his plate, lost in thought.

"Is something unsatisfactory, Mr. Gunnison?" a waiter asked.

"Hmm? Oh . . . no. Everything is fine. I've just been thinking about something."

"Can I bring you anything?"

"No. Not at the moment."

"Very good, sir."

Gunnison ate the rest of his meal without interruption, paid his bill, and walked back to his lonely house with his collar turned up and his hands thrust deep into his pockets.

Kenton . . . in Colorado.

Gunnison rolled the possibility over in his mind again and again and found it simply didn't fit. Kenton would not return without contacting him.

Not unless he was in trouble, major trouble, and didn't want to embroil his old friend and partner in it. Kenton was like that.

Nearly to his house, Gunnison stopped, sighed, and turned on his heel. His mind was churning; no point in going home just yet, because he couldn't relax if he did.

It was several blocks to the building full of renovated offices into which the *Illustrated American* had moved its operation only eight months before, but Gunnison walked them speedily despite his heavy supper. By the time he got to the office he'd worked off most of his tension.

He turned the key and entered the empty building. Not even a janitor around just now; Tuesday evenings the offices were empty except for the occasional late worker. The absence of lights in any windows indicated no one had stayed late tonight.

Gunnison didn't bother to light the hallway, walking it blindly by familiarity. He passed the little office that had been Kenton's. The door was slightly ajar, the room vaguely illuminated by the relatively brighter light outside. The desk was empty, the shelves still untouched and all Kenton's books in place despite the fact everyone believed him dead and the stuff should have been gone through long ago. Funny how nobody wanted to do it. Everybody liked having Kenton's office like it was. . . . It made it seem possible that he could reappear and come boisterously striding in like he always had. People around the office still talked in sentimental tones about this, like mourners at a funeral discussing how good the corpse looks.

Gunnison went to his office, lit and cranked up the light, and took a second look through the stack of mail he had received in the morning. He knew there was no letter from Charles Matthias, the pseudonym Kenton had chosen for his letters to Gunnison, but he looked anyway, just to be sure. Then he went to his father's office, the door of which always stood open, and examined his father's mail on the chance that a letter might have been delivered to the wrong Gunnison. Again, nothing.

Gunnison returned to his office and flopped down in his chair. He was tired, missed his wife, and was worried about Kenton. It had just been too long. He should have heard something by now.

The prospect of a journey to England seemed realer by the moment. But also daunting, especially as tired as he felt right now.

Gunnison leaned across his desk, resting his chin on the back of his crossed hands, then turned his head and rested his cheek instead. He closed his eyes.

CHAPTER

3

THE JAIL WAS SMALL, DIRTY, STINKING OF OLD COF-
fee and older cigar smoke. The town marshal who ran
the place had bleary eyes and the look of too much
liquor about him and eyed the Stetson-wearing Kenton with suspicion and Gunnison, who was clad in a
business suit, with something approaching disdain.

"Why should I let you see my prisoner?" the marshal said to Kenton. "What business is he of yours?"

"None at all, sir," Kenton replied with a smile. "But
he is a man who just robbed ten banks in succession
and killed five officers of the law in the process, and
it would be of tremendous interest to my readers if I
could sketch this scoundrel before he disappears into
the bowels of the courts and then on to the gallows."

"Ain't no concern of mine."

"Perhaps this is," Kenton said, reaching into his
pocket and pulling out a roll of bills. He tossed it onto
the desk in front of the marshal.

The marshal eyed it without words.

"I could arrest you for trying to bribe an officer."

"And I could report you to the town fathers for drinking on the job."

"Hell, they know I do it already."

"Take the money, Marshal. Give me fifteen minutes with the prisoner. That's all I ask."

The marshal reached over and took the money, pocketing it. He gestured with a toss of his head toward the big door leading into the rear cellblock.

Kenton and Gunnison followed the slightly staggering lawman through the door. The prisoner who was Kenton's target was in a cell on the left side of the cellblock; another prisoner, apparently drunk, was in the other.

"Who the hell is this?" growled the bank robber.

"His name's Brady Kenton. He's with the *Illustrated American*. This other fellow with him is his son."

"I'm not his son," Gunnison quickly corrected.

The marshal said nothing, just backed away from the cell and let Kenton go nearer to it. The bank robber was spread out across his bunk, staring at Kenton with a hateful gaze that it seemed to Gunnison was a little less authentic than it had been before he found out who Kenton was.

"I've heard of you, Kenton," he said. "I got no use for scribblers like you."

"America wants to know you, my friend," Kenton said, already beginning to sketch. "America is like that, you know. Crime and criminals intrigue us in the land of the free."

"I didn't give you no permission to sketch me."

Kenton just smiled and kept on sketching, and it was obvious that the man really didn't mind. It was an honor to be the subject of a sketch by the famous Brady Kenton.

It happened fast. The marshal made a strange, grunting sound. Gunnison turned and saw that the drunk in the cell behind him had put an arm through the bars and grabbed the marshal by the neck. His other hand was even then pulling free the Colt in the lawman's holster.

The lawman wrenched himself free, but the pistol remained in the prisoner's hand.

"What the—"

The pistol boomed, incredibly loud in the small space, the stench of expended gunpowder instantly burning Gunnison's nose. The marshal screeched as the bullet entered his thigh, dropping him to the floor at once.

Kenton had wheeled, letting his pad fall, and was making for the prisoner with the pistol before the man could withdraw too far back into the cell to be reached and before he could finish off the marshal with a second shot.

"No, Kenton!" Gunnison shouted.

But it was too late. The pistol went up, booming again, the bullet passing through Kenton's forehead and exiting the back of his head. . . .

Gunnison sat up with a grunt of alarm and stared wide-eyed across his desk.

A few moments later he was able to breathe again.

A dream. Thank God it had only been a dream!

But the events in the dream were based on a memory; they had been real, for the most part. The drunken and bribed marshal, the bank robber lounging on his cell bunk, the drunkard in the cell grabbing the pistol . . . all this had happened several years before, much as Gunnison had dreamed it.

But in the real-life version, Kenton had been able to grab the pistol away even before the prisoner could wound the marshal.

Gunnison closed his eyes and shuddered, unable to shake off the dream image of Kenton's head being shattered by that bullet.

Why would he dream such a thing?

He knew why. Because he was worried about Kenton. That maybe this time Kenton had run across a situation that he couldn't get the best of and it had gotten the best of him instead.

Gunnison rose, left the office building, and walked the lonely and dark way to his house, where he climbed into his cold bed and longed for his wife's return.

Gunnison arrived late at the office the following morning and was relieved that his father was not there to see it. Thank God for business travel!

But James Brooney, his father's unpleasant and nitpicking personal assistant, was there and stared at Gunnison with his usual cold arrogance. Word of this would get back to Gunnison's father. Brooney would make sure of it.

"Good morning, James," Gunnison said brightly as he passed the man who had become his in-office nemesis. He'd long since quit trying to win James over; clearly James viewed him as an heir unworthy to the throne he was soon to receive, and nothing Gunnison could do would change that. So now he just enjoyed what fun he could with James.

"Got something I want you to do for me today, James," he said in dead serious tones. "I want you to arrange to have the name of the magazine changed before the next edition."

"Change the . . . What do you mean?"

Gunnison paused at the door of his office and frowned at James as if he couldn't believe how dense the man was. "I said I want the name of the magazine changed. Right away."

"Sir, you can't change the name of the magazine without your father's permission!"

"Who says I can't? I'm going to be the publisher soon enough. . . . Can't I call it what I want?"

"You aren't the publisher yet, sir."

"Maybe I am. Maybe I got a letter from my father telling me that now I'm the man in charge."

"May I see this letter?"

"Who are you to make demands on me, James? I'm the one in charge here! And I want to name my magazine . . . Let me see. . . . How about . . . *The Flatulent's Friend*? That'll do. Go have a nameplate designed right away."

James, who had absolutely no sense of humor and was extremely prudish, reddened nearly to the shade of a tomato. "Sir . . . I can't do such a thing! It's atrocious. . . . Your father will . . . Sir, you can't mean it!"

"Of course I can't mean it, James. I'm just joking with you. When are you going to learn to laugh a little?" Gunnison swept into his office and closed the door, smiling to himself.

CHAPTER

4

THE EXCHANGE HAD BEEN OVERHEARD AND MADE the rounds of office gossip, causing much sneaking laughter at James's expense.

Gunnison, though, didn't much enjoy the levity, because he was immersed in worry again about what had happened to Kenton. It was terribly hard to know that Kenton had faked his death and not be able to tell anyone . . . especially now that he was worried. There was no one in whom he could confide, no one from whom he could seek advice. Kenton had made him vow not to tell anyone, even his wife. He'd kept his promise . . . mostly. Roxanne did not know Kenton still lived.

But Gunnison had told one other person. It had simply been impossible not to do so, for the sake of his own mental health.

Perhaps there were steps he could take toward finding his answers without further compromising the promise he had made. He thought hard, then stood and went to the shelf for his notepad. He sat down and put his feet upon his desk and began to write, balancing the pad on his crossed legs.

Fifteen minutes later, James lowered the temperature of the room simply by entering the door.

"You're working, I presume, on the introductory piece for the next edition?"

"It'll get done, James."

"It was due, you are aware, three days ago."

"It'll get done."

"Your father entrusted the job to you . . . a job on which he never ran late."

"It'll get done."

"So that is what you're working on?"

"No. I'm writing your dismissal letter. It's very satisfying work."

"You . . . my . . . uh, are you joking with me again, sir?"

"Go ponder on it awhile. Close the door as you leave."

James turned and walked away, chin up and steps a little too fast. He closed the door . . . hard. Gunnison shook his head. Poor James! He'd be glad to be friendlier to him if only he would quit being so blasted uppity.

James was right that Gunnison was behind on his work, and no doubt he would hear about it when his father returned from his travels. But just now Gunnison didn't care. He was writing a letter to Scotland Yard, inquiring about Kenton. . . .

But as he wrote, his enthusiasm faded. A letter would take a long time to reach England and a longer time again to be answered, if ever it was. This was merely an exercise in activity for the sake of feeling better, and that was all.

Gunnison ripped the paper off the pad, wadded it, and threw it across the room into the rubbish bin, just as the office door opened again and Billy Connery stuck his head in.

"You know, Alex, I've been thinking of coming up with some sort of game in which the object would be throwing a ball into a basket of some sort."

"Nobody would be interested, Billy."

Billy Connery, Irish-born illustrator who was five years Gunnison's junior and an employee of the *Illustrated American* since mere days after Kenton's supposed death. It hadn't taken long for him to become Gunnison's closest friend . . . and not much longer to become the one living person to whom Gunnison had betrayed the truth about Kenton's "death."

Connery entered the office and closed the door behind him. "Having trouble finishing that introductory column, are you?"

"I've not started it."

"What? But it was due days ago!"

"I know that, Billy."

"Sorry . . . it's not my place to point out deadlines to my own boss."

"That's not why I'm irritable. I'm just worried."

"About your wife?"

"No . . . although I do miss her, very badly."

Connery lowered his volume significantly. "About Kenton, then."

"Yes. It's been too long, Billy. I should have heard from him by now."

Connery looked at him seriously. "You should tell your father."

"I can't. Kenton made me promise firmly. He was very specific that my father in particular was not to know he's alive."

"Why?"

"I don't know. He has a strong sense of duty to my father. . . . Maybe having Father believe he is dead gives him a sense of freedom from that duty, so he can concentrate all his attention on finding Victoria. Whatever the reason, I made a promise to him."

"You already broke it once, when you told me."

"I know. I don't claim to be consistent. I just don't know what to do, Billy."

"You're going to have to go after him, I believe."

"I've been thinking that."

"You could probably find a professional pretext for going, so that no one would know the true reason for it. And you could take your Irish illustrator friend with you."

"You'd want to come?"

"It would be a welcome trip for me. And I'm the only person around who can help you, because I'm the only other one besides you who knows."

"I heard something last night that surprised me," Kenton said. "I was told that Kenton has been seen in Colorado, in some little mining town I don't know the name of."

"It's not surprising. As famous as Kenton's face is,

there's bound to be people thinking they see him. They say everyone has someone else who looks like them."

"Maybe that's all it is. But I'd heard something similar from someone else earlier."

"But it's impossible. Kenton would have contacted you had he returned to the United States."

"Yes . . . unless something was very wrong. Unless he had to hide so thoroughly that he couldn't. Unless things had gone so badly that he cut himself off from everyone he knew before."

"These are some substantial suppositions to be making on the basis of some rumors, Alex."

"I realize that. But I've got a bad feeling, Billy. Something is wrong . . . and somehow I've got to find out what it is."

"It does seem something should have been heard by now, I do confess."

"I think maybe I really will have to go to England."

"If you do, I truly would like to go with you."

"We'll see. I don't think I'll make any big decisions. Not until Roxanne gets home."

"You'll be glad to see her, eh?" Connery smiled brightly and winked.

"I will. And not just for the reasons you're obviously thinking about."

CHAPTER

5

THE TRAIN CAME TO A HALT WITH AN EAR-BUFFETING metallic screech and the piercing hiss of steaming brakes. Alex Gunnison stood on the platform so excited he was hardly able to restrain himself from dancing.

She descended, wearing her beauty like a robe, and he went to her nearly on a run, throwing his arms around her and kissing her right there in the midst of the crowd.

"Welcome back, Roxanne!" he said. "You don't know how I've missed you!"

She squeezed him until he couldn't breathe. "Of course I know. You think I didn't miss you just as badly?"

"Then you should have come home sooner."

"I couldn't cut the visit short. It had been too long since the last one for me to do that."

"I know. But I can't help but be selfish. I want you all to myself."

She gave him the kind of smile that could still melt

him despite their several years together. "I'm glad. Now tell me: how are the cats?"

"Fine. I'll bet you thought about them more than about me."

"Nonsense! Did you water the plants every day?"

"Of course."

"Oh, Alex, can we go to Barrigan's tonight? I'd love to sit back and relax and enjoy a good meal and just have the chance to look at you for a while."

"A marvelous idea. I'd already thought of doing that even before you mentioned it. I ate there while you were gone. . . . The place isn't the same without you."

He carried her bags in one hand and held her arm in the other, happy to be with her again. He put aside thoughts of Brady Kenton and decided, almost unconsciously, not to mention tonight his upcoming trip to England. There would be time for that later.

Brady Kenton had intruded into the life of the Gunnisons for years. Tonight he would not.

But as Gunnison and his wife were finishing their meal, lingering over dessert and coffee, Brady Kenton did intrude.

"Oh, I just remembered . . ." Roxanne said suddenly. "The strangest thing . . . Wait a moment. . . ." She began digging in her bag.

"What are you up to?" Gunnison asked.

"Wait. . . . Ah, yes, here it is." She pulled a ragged envelope from her bag and laid it on the table in front of her husband's plate.

Gunnison picked it up. "It appears to be an envelope addressed to the Buckeye Cafe in Culvertown, Colorado."

"Look on the back."

Gunnison flipped it over and stared in silence.

"Whose work would you say that was, Alex?"

Gunnison was gazing at a casual pencil study of a man in a vest and sleeve garters, carrying a food-laden tray.

"This looks like Kenton's work."

"Yes."

"Where did you get it?"

"I found it in that cafe, the Buckeye."

"What were you doing in Culvertown?"

"It was a side trip. I went with one of Aunt Karen's friends to visit her brother there. We ate at this cafe, and I found the envelope on the table."

"It's astonishing! I've never seen such a good imitation of his work. Or maybe it isn't an imitation at all. Maybe this is some old sketch done by Kenton years ago."

"The man in the sketch is a waiter in the cafe . . . the same waiter who waited on our table."

"Well, so he's worked there several years."

"He was wearing the same clothes as you see in the drawing."

"So the cafe has a uniform code of dress for its employees."

"Look at the postmark date, Alex."

Gunnison flipped it over. The postmark was only days old.

To his mind came the words of the man who had approached him in Barrigan's: *My brother Cordell swears, absolutely swears, that he saw Brady Kenton himself not a week ago, in Colorado . . . says he knows for a fact this was none other than the man.*

Gunnison was now almost sure that Brady Kenton really was back in the United States, in Colorado . . . yet he had made no contact.

Roxanne looked closely at her husband. "Alex . . . should I not have showed you that sketch? You look upset."

"It's just that . . . it's a bit of a shock, seeing what appears to be an authentic Kenton drawing, but which couldn't be."

"I know," she replied. "It's impossible. I inquired of the proprietor about the sketch, wondering if he knew who had left it. He didn't, but a waiter gave a description of a man who sounded remarkably like Kenton himself. He said the man had dined alone and seemed melancholy."

Kenton . . . dining alone. Perhaps he had failed in his quest to bring back Victoria and had been so depressed he had gone into hiding in a remote Colorado mining town. It wouldn't be the first time Kenton had gone off to hide and lick his wounds.

Gunnison wondered if Kenton was drinking again. And where was Rachel Frye, his daughter? She'd gone with him to England. Had she not returned?

Questions abounded, demanding answers, and Gunnison sat staring off into the dark corner of the restaurant, feeling frustration and restlessness rise because just now those answers could not be found.

"Alex, did you hear what I said?"

"Of course I did. You were talking about this sketch."

"No . . . I was telling you how eager I am to get you home and alone."

He smiled. "Intriguing, I must say. How could I have missed that?"

Gunnison folded the envelope and put it in his pocket, determined to forget about Kenton for the rest of the evening.

He doubted he would succeed. The questions were just too big to be forgotten.

When Alex Gunnison left the house to go to work the next morning, Roxanne stood in the doorway and waved him away with a bright smile on her face.

As soon as he was out of sight, though, the smile vanished, and she closed the door with her heart heavy and her brow creased by a frown.

Something was wrong with Alex. Something was so on his mind that it was pushing her out of his attention.

She wondered desperately what it could be and why he would not tell her about it.

That sketch on the envelope, maybe. Perhaps that had disturbed him in some way. She wished she hadn't shown it to him.

Returning to the bedroom, she looked on the bureau where Alex had placed the envelope last night. The envelope was gone. He'd taken it with him to the office.

CHAPTER
6

BILLY CONNERY STOOD BY THE WINDOW, LOOKING at the sketch where the light was brightest.

"Amazing indeed," he said. "You know Brady Kenton's work better than any man alive, Alex, but if I was asked to judge, I would have to say that this is indeed his sketching."

"You're right on both scores: I do know his work better than anyone does, and I can vouch for that as an authentic Kenton sketch."

"Which means the man is indeed back in the country and apparently spending his time in Colorado."

"Yes, but in hiding, it would seem. If not in hiding, at least cutting himself off from his friends."

"Why would he do such a thing?"

"He would do it only if something was very wrong. He's hiding because he must."

"Or because he wants to. Because he is in some sort of despair," Connery said.

"Yes. That could be. So what now?"

"Well, if it's my advice you're asking, I say throw

aside my earlier encouragement for you to go to England and replace it with encouragement to go to Colorado."

"My thoughts exactly. Colorado it is."

"We can perhaps come up with some pretext . . . a story we are to do about something or another. The shepherds of the Colorado mountains, perhaps."

"Already did it, back in '79."

"We'll think of something."

"I gather you're planning to go as well."

"Of course! Who else can help you more? And if we're to make the pretense of going to produce a story and art, it would be expected that I would go along anyway."

"That's true."

"And as I noted earlier, there's no one else you could go with who wouldn't become a millstone around your neck, because there's no one else but me who knows Kenton is still alive."

"Maybe I should take Roxanne. Maybe it's time I told her the truth."

"Kenton told you not to."

"Yes. But Kenton has always thought he could run every aspect of my life for me. I'm getting tired of having to keep a secret from my own wife just because he wanted me to, for some inexplicable reason."

"That's your judgment to make, Alex. You've already taken me into your confidence on the matter. If you want to tell your wife as well, that's your choice."

Gunnison did want to tell her yet also didn't. He knew Roxanne. She would be very displeased that he'd kept the secret from her as long as he had and would let him know it. She'd also never be able to keep it quiet, he feared. Willingly or unwillingly, she'd let it slip. And she would resent that he'd told Billy Connery before he told her.

"I think I'll hold quiet for now," he said. "But she'll think it strange that I've gone to Colorado right in the wake of her just getting back from there. She'll know it's because of the envelope."

"Then perhaps you shouldn't keep quiet."

But Gunnison was thinking hard all at once. "I'll tell her I'm going to find the man who did the sketch in hopes of hiring him because of his obvious skills."

"In other words, that you're looking for someone to replace yours truly."

"Don't get sensitive on me, Billy. We both know it's just a cover story."

"Shall I begin to make the arrangements?"

"Don't take this wrong, Billy, but if I'm going to Colorado ostensibly to find another artist, it wouldn't make sense for me to be taking you along."

Connery was crestfallen. "I don't want to be left out of this one, Alex. I'm as intrigued by this as you are."

"I understand. But I think it's going to be just me this time around."

Connery returned the envelope to Gunnison's desk with a sigh. "Very well, boss and governor. If you want Billy staying behind, Billy stays behind."

"Don't be peeved at me, Billy."

"Peeved? Don't know the meaning of the word,"

Connery said tightly, leaving the room without another glance at Gunnison.

The task of sorting and distributing the heap of mail that came almost daily to the offices of the *Illustrated American* was the prized and much-protected duty of Joe Stamps. Stamps was a somber man in his forties who looked fifteen years older than he was and whose mind had never developed beyond that of a boy. Gunnison's father happened to be a tenderhearted and progressive man who held the unusual view that society was obliged by common decency to provide a place and livelihood for those whose mental situations made it pretty much impossible for them to do so on their own.

He had hired Stamps shortly after the *Illustrated American* had moved to its current office building. Stamps had initially roused concerns among the less progressive-minded staff members, but time had proven him to be a good and reliable man with a strong sense of duty.

Stamps took his job very seriously, and on the rare occasion he made a mistake, distress almost overwhelmed him. When he entered Alex Gunnison's office, Gunnison knew at once that something had gone wrong.

"What is it, Joe?" Gunnison asked.

"I've made a mistake," Stamps replied, his voice tight. "I know how important it is for letters to reach you fast, and I try my best to make sure they do. But sometimes things fall off the table in the mailroom.

Sometimes even when I look, I'll miss them if they fall in behind something. I'm sorry."

"So you've found a letter that had fallen behind a table?"

"Yes, sir. It should have come to you a week ago. I'm sorry that it's wrinkled and dirty."

Stamps extended a crumpled envelope, smudged with grime.

"Thank you, Joe."

"I'll try not to let it happen again, Mr. Gunnison. Please don't take away my job."

"No one is going to take away your job over one lost letter."

"Thank you, sir. I really do appreciate it."

"Fine. You're welcome."

"I only wish I had looked sooner behind that table. Then maybe it wouldn't have been lost at all. From now on I'm going to look behind the table every day. No, twice a day."

"Good."

Gunnison was studying the return address of the envelope in his hand. It was that of a hospital in New York. He'd hoped it would be the identifying code name and address he and Kenton had worked out.

"Thank you again for not taking away my job, Mr. Gunnison."

"Fine. You can go about your work now, Joe."

Joe thanked Gunnison yet again as he headed out the door.

Gunnison tore the envelope open. The letter was written in a nearly illegible hand, clearly the product of someone working in a hurry. He had to read slowly just to make out what it said.

Once he was through reading it, he laid the letter on the desk and stared at it a moment. Then he picked it up, folded it and placed it in his pocket, and set out at once to find Billy Connery.

CHAPTER

7

BILLY CONNERY LOWERED THE LETTER AND frowned thoughtfully. "This Rachel Frye, that's Brady Kenton's daughter, right?"

"Yes."

"And she went to England with Kenton."

"She did."

"Then how has she come to end up in a hospital in New York?"

"A good question."

"Perhaps we can wire the hospital and find out."

"I intend to do that. I expect we'll find she's still there. It's a charity-based hospital, the letterhead indicates, so I doubt they'd throw her into the streets."

"I wonder if Kenton knows she's there?"

"I can't believe he would. He would never stand by while his flesh and blood was in some kind of medical crisis."

"This seems to be a common refrain."

"What do you mean?"

"This thing of 'Kenton would never' do this or do

that. Kenton would never come back to the United States without letting you know. But obviously he has. Kenton would never let his own daughter languish alone in a hospital far from him. But again, it appears he has."

"I can assure you, there has to be a reason for whatever he's doing. I've known Kenton a long time. I know the man he is."

"Unless the man he is now isn't the man you've known. Something might have happened to change him."

Gunnison couldn't deny this possibility. Kenton had a history of occasional lapses into despair and drinking, and at such times he would become different than he was in better times. Kenton's bad periods were inevitably triggered by negative events—severe disappointments, failures, personal crises of one kind or another.

Gunnison was fairly sure now that Kenton's quest to find his wife in England had failed. This blow, which would be the worst of his life, might have driven him further than ever before into drinking and self-isolation.

He had to find Kenton and help him, or Kenton might not be around much longer to be found at all.

"What will you do now?" Connery asked, handing the letter back to Gunnison.

"Go to New York."

"I'd like to go with you."

"No. I have another job for you. I want you to go to Colorado in my place."

"Really? To look for Kenton?"

"Yes. I need to go to both Colorado and New York, and clearly I can't pull that one off."

"You know that I've never met Kenton."

"No, but you've seen more than enough pictures of him. Besides, it might be good to have someone looking for him whom he's never met. If he saw me before I saw him and if he didn't want me to find him, he'd simply disappear. You'll be able to find him without rousing suspicion . . . I hope."

Connery, beaming, pumped Gunnison's hand. "Thank you, Alex. I'll not let you down. If he's there to be found, I'll find him."

"You'll have to be careful how you proceed. Kenton is clever, and if he's trying to hide, he'll not be easy to locate."

"It doesn't appear to me that he's been particularly clever," Connery replied. "He did a sketch and simply left it in a cafe to be found."

"I admit that does seem careless, if he's trying to stay in hiding. But maybe it was a simple oversight on his part."

"I will be careful. And if Kenton is in some sort of bad situation, I'll do all I can to help him."

"Watch out for yourself as well. Kenton may be hiding because he's in danger. If you find him, you could be in danger, too."

"What kind of danger?"

"I don't know. All I know is that Dr. David Kevington is a determined and dangerous man, willing to do whatever it takes to gain and keep what he wants.

He kidnapped Kenton's wife years ago and hid her away like his personal treasure. If Kenton managed to get her away from him, Kevington would probably know no limits in how he'd react, trying to get her back."

Connery pondered this a moment. "Kenton could be hiding from Dr. Kevington, then."

"Maybe. We can't know until we find him. But, Billy . . . if you do find Kenton, please be sure that you don't accidentally help somebody else find him, too."

Connery took this in thoughtfully, then nodded. "I will indeed proceed with great caution. And you do the same."

"I will." Gunnison shook the letter. "I wish this told me the reason that Rachel is hospitalized."

"Whatever it is, it must be no small thing, to keep her nearly unconscious for weeks."

"It doesn't even tell us whether it was illness or injury. This is a hurriedly written letter."

"Probably written by a physician with more work than he can handle. Can you imagine how mystifying, and frustrating, it must have been to have a patient who for weeks was unable to reveal who she was or who to contact about her?"

"I wonder if Kenton knows where she is?"

"Well, if he doesn't, you can tell him when you find him. I doubt he knows."

"How will you explain your New York journey to Roxanne?"

"I think maybe the time has come to do something radical."

"Tell her the truth?"

"Exactly."

Connery's living quarters were small, cheap, second-story, and within easy walking distance of the *Illustrated American*. Typical of an unmarried young male, he lived amid his own mess, clothing strewn all about and the remnants of three-day-old meals still lingering on molding plates in dusty corners.

He usually was oblivious to the clutter, but at the moment it was a problem because he was trying to pack, which involved having to do some serious digging amid the smutty heaps. With every atrocity he uncovered he grew more disgusted at his own slovenly ways.

One of these days he'd do better, he vowed to himself. Especially when he had a woman to impress. At the moment, there was none. Connery's romantic efforts of late had been faltering failures. But maybe, someday, there'd be a knock on his door, he'd open it, find some lovely creature on the other side, needing directions or help carrying something or to borrow a cup of flour, and a great romance would be born. It was a common fantasy for Billy Connery, though so far nothing remotely like it had happened.

There was a knock on the door. "I'll be!" Connery muttered. "Wouldn't you know she'd show up right when I'm about to leave for Colorado!"

But it wasn't the girl of his dreams. It was exactly

who he knew it would be: J. R. Randwick, who lived in the rooms across the hall. He played a dual role in Connery's life: friend and annoyer.

"Come in, J. R. What brings you over this evening?"

"Hearing you bumping around. What are you doing?"

"What does it look like? I'm packing."

"Getting ready to travel, eh?"

"You know, you ought to go into detective work, J. R. You're wasted back in the bowels of that bakery."

"Where are you going?"

"West. Colorado. Some isolated mining town called Culvertown."

"Big story, huh?"

"You might say."

"Alex Gunnison going with you?"

"No. This one's on my own."

"What? You're writing the story, too, not just drawing?"

"No, I'm not writing."

"So you'll just be publishing pictures, no story?"

"Questions, questions. You're full of them, J. R."

J. R. wandered over to Connery's table and tore a hunk from a loaf of bread there. Connery glowered at him. "Don't you have food of your own?"

"Sure. I just like this bread you've got."

"You should. You baked it yesterday."

"That's why it's so good. Hey, let me go with you to Colorado."

"What? You've got to work, my friend."

"Nope. The bakery is closed for two weeks. They're rebuilding the whole inside of it while the boss is off taking care of his sick father. I've got free time, and plenty of money saved up. I'm going with you."

"You can't, J. R."

"Why? Will I break your concentration while you scribble your pictures?"

"This is a different kind of a trip. I'm not going to be drawing."

"Then what?"

"None of your business, but I'll be looking for someone." There was a moment of inner warning: *You're about to say too much.* But what did it really matter? J. R. was harmless, and if he didn't give him solid explanations about why he couldn't tag along on his journey, J. R. would push and push and push some more.

"Who you looking for?"

"A man. A missing fellow. Somebody that Mr. Gunnison wants to find."

"Why not just hire a detective?"

"There's reasons."

"Aha! Secrecy. Something sneaky and covert. Now I know I've got to go with you."

"J. R., you can't. I'm serious about that. I've been given an assignment to carry out for Alex Gunnison, and I have to keep it quiet. This is a very important thing."

Connery noticed the way J. R. was looking at him,

intrigue mixed with jealousy. Despite himself, Connery felt a boyish surging of his ego and added an extra detail he would later wish he hadn't: "You might say I'm going to see if we can't bring a man back from the dead."

"What?"

"Never mind."

"No. You tell me what that means. You can't throw out something like that and not tell me what you're talking about."

"I can't say any more. I wish I could."

"You're looking for somebody who's dead?"

"No."

"Somebody who people think is dead, then."

Connery said nothing.

"That's it! You're looking to find somebody who people think is dead. Maybe somebody pretending to be dead."

"You better go, J. R."

"I've figured it out! Who is it? Tell me!"

Connery would not tell, though J. R. prodded and probed until Connery could hardly stand it. When J. R. left, he was angry and frustrated.

Connery finished packing and knew he'd made a mistake. Probably nothing would come of it, but he'd be sure not to let Alex Gunnison know what he'd just done.

He'd be much more careful from here on out.

It took some time for her to grasp what he told her, and when she did, her reaction made Gunnison wonder if he'd done the right thing in opening his mouth.

"Let me understand this," she said, a little icily. "All this time, Brady Kenton has been alive. The *Illustrated American* published a big story that was . . . a lie. Memorial tributes poured in from everyone from your father through the vice president of the United States . . . all for a man who really wasn't dead at all."

"That's pretty much it."

"All because he asked you to."

"Roxanne, you have to look at it from Kenton's side, and from mine. You know how important his quest for Victoria was to him. Most people scoffed at it and thought him a fool for believing his wife might still be alive . . . but he was right. By letting the world think he was dead, he had the freedom to go to England and seriously look for her. I had to agree to his request, Roxanne."

"But you lied to me, along with everyone else."

"He made me promise. He didn't want me to tell anyone at all. Only Rachel Frye, a Texas Ranger named Frank Turner, and I knew Kenton was still alive. He wanted to keep it that way. . . . Even to tell just one person opened the door to the truth getting out."

"But I'm your wife, Alex! We're not supposed to have secrets between one another."

"I'm sorry. I didn't know you'd react so strongly."

"It's just that the vows we made to each other when we were married were more important than the vow you made to Kenton."

"Oh, come now, Roxanne. . . . Are you trying to

tell me that there's nothing you know that I don't know? That you've never kept anything secret from me?"

"That's exactly what I'm telling you."

"That's hard to believe."

She was obviously offended. "It makes me wonder what else you're keeping from me."

"What?"

"I've wondered at times . . . I'm sorry to say this, Alex . . . but I did sometimes wonder if it was really Brady Kenton who kept you away from me for so much time over all those years. I wondered if you were away from me because you wanted to be."

"Roxanne!"

"And I wondered if there were . . . other women."

Gunnison wished now he'd not told her the truth about Kenton. He'd not had any notion that it would be such a catalyst for all this anger.

"There were never other women. Never. I've been forever faithful to you."

She stared at him, eyes beginning to fill.

"Roxanne, what can I say to you? Do you not believe me?"

Her lip trembled.

"Roxanne, I love you. I would die before I would be unfaithful to you."

Tears came. She went to him and put her arms around him. "I know. I know."

"Did you really doubt me?"

"No. I'm sorry. I was just angry that you'd keep such a secret from me."

"I hope you can understand why I felt that I had to."

"I do."

"And in the end, I did tell you. I broke my vow to Kenton today. Just like I broke it when I told Billy Connery." Gunnison decided not to reveal to her that he'd told Connery the truth months ago. Given her reactions so far, it was best to let her think he'd told Connery only today. He'd be sure to tell Connery not to say anything around Roxanne that would indicate otherwise.

"Yes," she said. "I'm sorry I acted like I did."

"Forget all about it." He hugged her. "You are glad to know that Kenton didn't really die, aren't you?"

"Of course . . . but I hope it doesn't mean that he'll come back and take you off on the road with him again."

"That won't happen. My days apart from you are finished. But I do have to go away one more time, just this once. I've got to go to New York."

"Because of the letter . . . Rachel Frye."

"That's right."

"Yes, you must go. But not alone. I'm going with you."

"With me? Roxanne . . . there's a chance, just a chance, that there may be some danger involved. Kenton may be hiding because someone is after him, or maybe Victoria. If so, they might be after Rachel as well."

"If there's danger, that's all the more reason for me to go. I want to look out for you."

"I'd rather have you safe at home."

"Has it crossed your mind, Husband, that if some-one is trying to find Kenton, it won't take them long to come looking around Kenton's workplace, and his friends?"

Gunnison hadn't thought about that. It made sense, and scared him.

"They might watch this very house, Alex, thinking that Kenton might show up here."

Gunnison nodded. "I think you may have a point, Roxanne."

"I'm going with you to New York."

"Yes. You are."

"Will Billy be safe going to Colorado alone?"

"I hope so. . . . I'll talk to him again before he leaves and tell him to watch out. He's excited about his assignment and already packing even though his train won't leave until day after tomorrow."

"When will we leave?"

"Tomorrow morning. I want to get to Rachel Frye as quickly as possible."

CHAPTER

8

BY THE TIME THE TRAIN CARRYING BILLY CONNERY toward Colorado had left Missouri, the excitement of travel and adventure had given way to worry.

Connery sat by the window, staring out at the passing landscape, trying to figure out just how he'd go about locating Brady Kenton. His destination was Culvertown, one of the many Colorado mountain communities that had made the transition from mining camp to town. Though Connery had never been to Culvertown itself, he'd traveled once before in the Rockies and knew what to expect: a rough-and-ready town with a narrow main street, a few good brick edifices mixed with plenty of structures made of lumber, and with the mountains all around scarred from mining and covered over with rough miners' huts like pox scabs on a sick patient. And since Culvertown was still an active mining center, the population probably would be large and fluid, people coming and going literally by the day.

How would he start to locate Brady Kenton in such

a place? And come to think of it, how would he manage to make inquiries without looking like he was a candidate for an asylum? *Pardon me, sir, but I'm looking for the celebrity journalist Brady Kenton.... Yes, I know you read all about his death.... Yes, it was a sad thing. You haven't by chance seen the late Mr. Kenton on the streets recently, have you?*

Oh, well. He'd figure out a way. He pulled the envelope from his pocket and studied the drawing on the back of it. As an illustrator himself, he found it impossible not to be both admiring and envious of Kenton's skill. With only a few strokes of a pencil he could capture depth, character, the play of light and shadow. *Someday I'll be as good as that,* Connery promised himself.

As nervous as this whole undertaking made him, there was one aspect of it that he looked forward to very much: he would get to actually meet Brady Kenton, the man whose work had inspired him to become an illustrator himself. He'd wept when he learned of Kenton's "death," it having been a goal of his to someday meet the man.

Now he'd get to fulfill that goal . . . if he could find Kenton.

He could only hope that his reception would not be hostile. Having gone into hiding, Kenton would probably not be pleased to be found.

Connery was asleep when the train finally pulled into the station where he was to disembark. He lifted his head, tipped back the bowler hat he'd pulled low across his brows, and blinked a few times until his vision cleared. He'd been sleeping soundly, dreaming about Ireland, reliving a boyhood conversation he'd had with his grandfather, who was now laid away these several years beneath the green Irish sod.

Connery adjusted his hat, picked up his bag, and secretly patted his pocket to make sure the roll of bills he'd been provided by Alex Gunnison was still there. Alex had funded this assignment informally, avoiding an official expense report and simply forwarding Connery cash from one of the *Illustrated American* accounts. Gunnison was not about to go on record as having assigned someone to go search for a dead man.

Connery departed the train and took a deep breath of fresh mountain air . . . as fresh, anyway, as the air can be beside a smoking train in a mining town rich with belching chimneys. After having resided on a train since St. Louis, it felt tremendously good to stretch his legs and move about.

The first order of business was food, and he found this in the nearest restaurant. Eating at a table by a window, he watched people pass and tried to spot a place where he could obtain a horse. He was not yet at Culvertown. It lay high in the mountains, not yet touched by a railroad spur, though one was even now being constructed.

To reach Culvertown, Connery would have to either catch a coach or rent a horse and saddle. Gunnison had suggested the latter, in that having a horse would give Connery freedom of movement in and around Culvertown. If Kenton was hiding, he might be in some old miner's cabin out in the mountains somewhere.

After fifteen minutes of striding around the town, Connery located a livery and shopped for a rental horse. He encountered an unpleasant surprise: the proprietor of the livery apparently had no use for Irishmen, and Connery had enough of a brogue to mark him as one. When the man refused to lower the price to anything approaching reasonable, Connery stormed off in a huff and spent another thirty minutes looking for another livery.

This time he put on his best flat American accent and quickly took possession of a fine roan at a reasonable cost. The horse came with assurances that it was a horse accustomed to the thin air of the mountains and would serve him well as he headed up to the higher altitudes around Culvertown. The saddle was old but comfortable to both horse and rider and for a little extra came equipped with a rifle sleeve. Connery strapped his bag on the back of the saddle, thanked and tipped the liveryman, and rode out onto the sunny street.

One more stop awaited before he began the last leg of his journey. He rode to the nearest gun shop and purchased a used Winchester rifle and a new Colt pistol, with a shoulder holster for the latter and ammunition for both weapons. He felt very extravagant, spending so much in one day, but Gunnison had given him clear instructions to do all these things and not worry about the cost. The *Illustrated American* could afford it, and it was important that Connery be well armed and well mounted.

There were two other men in the gun shop when Connery made his purchases. They were examining rifles in a glass case, seemingly paying little heed to Connery, but when he pulled out his roll of bills he did get the feeling that they noticed it. He promised himself to be more careful in the future about showing the amount of money he had on him.

He left the gun shop and slid his Winchester into the saddle boot. A perfect fit. Connery swung into the saddle and rode to the next corner, pausing long enough to inspect a pole on which various slabs had been nailed, with arrows pointing in the directions of other towns in the vicinity. He found the indicator for Culvertown and rode off in that direction.

He did not notice that the pair in the gun shop had emerged and watched his departure. After he rounded the corner and was out of sight, they glanced at each other, speaking quickly and low, and trotted off to a nearby hitching post where their own mounts waited.

CHAPTER

9

ON THE ROAD WITH BRADY KENTON, ALEX GUNNI-son had spent many days freezing in blizzards or roasting in the sun and many nights sleeping in barns, on the ground, in tepees, shepherd's wagons, line camp cabins, and every other kind of rough shelter imaginable. Now that his professional life was more settled, it was difficult to adjust to the trappings of his family's wealth. The money and mansions had been there a long time. . . . Alex Gunnison simply hadn't been situated to take much advantage of them until Kenton's "death" substantially ended his wandering life.

He was seated now in a passenger car on an east-bound train, Roxanne at his side. Surrounding them were common passengers—cowboys, sodbusters, traveling salesmen, all sorts. Babies cried and men smoked smelly cigars that made Roxanne cough.

"Alex," she said to him, "how long are we going to sit here?"

"Oh, I don't know. However long we want."

"But we've got a car of our own to go to. There's no crowds, no noise, no cigar smoke. There are padded chairs instead of these benches. Why can't we go there?"

"I don't feel right there. It's too fancy, too uppity."

"Then the *Illustrated American* has paid to have your father's own private car joined to this train for no reason."

"The *Illustrated American* can afford it. And it hasn't been wasted. We slept in it last night, didn't we?" He paused. "Frankly, Roxanne, that car is my father's domain, not mine. I just don't feel right being in it. I'm used to more rugged modes of travel."

"Only because Brady Kenton always insisted on roughing it."

"Not always. At times Kenton loved his luxury. But he always said that to practice good journalism, he had to be among the people, not cut off from them. So he looked for the cheap hotels and the cheap railroad tickets and the roughest barrooms. That's where he found his best stories."

Roxanne took a fresh faceful of cigar smoke and hacked for half a minute. "Alex, I think I should note that we're not looking for stories. We're simply traveling to New York. There's no particular reason to be 'among the people' this trip . . . especially when they smoke cigars as smelly as the one that man over there is afflicting us with."

He smiled at her. "I'm sorry, Roxanne. Old habits die hard, and I've not been thoughtful. Tell you what:

why don't you go on back to our private car? I'll join you shortly."

"Come with me now! How can you abide the smell of that cigar?"

"Actually, I'm thinking of smoking one myself."

She frowned. Gunnison had recently taken up the habit of smoking a cigar a day, and she didn't like it. Nor would she accept his explanation that his father had actually suggested he smoke more often, because it made him seem more professional, more one of the upper crust of the magazine world. In the publishing world, anyone who was anyone smoked cigars.

"If you're going to sit here and add to the foulness in the air, then indeed I will go back alone," she said. "Perhaps you will join me later . . . after the smell has had time to fade off your clothing."

She leaned over and kissed him on the cheek. "Enjoy your cigar . . . in that you evidently prefer the company of tobacco to that of your devoted wife."

"You're very unfair, you know."

"Yes, indeed." She patted his knee, rose, and was gone.

He was halfway through his cigar when she was back again.

"Roxanne? You look pale. . . . Is something wrong?"

"Alex, we're not alone on this train."

"Of course we're not alone."

"No! What I mean is, someone is on this train because of us. Someone is following us."

"Why do you think so?"

"Because when I went back to our car, I saw some-one trying to enter. I stopped and watched long enough to be sure.... I sat down in one of the empty seats in the passenger car and watched him at least two minutes. It was only when the conductor walked through that he stopped. He pretended to be looking for something he'd dropped at our door. He came walking back through the passenger car, but he didn't see me. There was a newspaper there and I lifted it and pretended to read, and hid my face as he went by."

Gunnison's heart was pounding faster. He dropped the cigar onto the dirty floor and crushed it out. The car swayed and rumbled.

"Maybe it was just a common thief, trying to break into the nearest private railroad car."

"I don't think so. I saw the same man in St. Louis, as we were getting aboard."

"It's not that surprising.... He's on the same train as we are, and he had to get on somewhere."

"He was looking at you before we boarded.... I noticed it at the time but didn't think much of it. You are becoming better known in the city."

"Where is this man now?"

"Not in here ... but he must have passed through."

"Several people have passed through here; I paid no heed to them."

"Let's go back to our car. I don't feel safe here."

"I'd like to get a look at this fellow you saw. Maybe have a word with him."

"No! No, don't do it. I'm too scared for you to do that right now. But why would anyone be following us?" she asked.

"Who knows? Perhaps he is just a common thief after all, and thought I looked wealthy enough to be worth robbing."

"Could it have anything to do with Kenton?"

"Surely not. I can't see how. I mean, nobody knows what we're up to except ourselves and Billy."

"Maybe somebody else is trying to find Kenton, somebody bad. Maybe Kenton is in hiding because of that. And maybe whoever it is decided that Kenton might get in touch with you because you are his publisher and his old partner."

"This is an awful lot to surmise just from somebody trying to break into our car. I'm sure that robbery in private railroad cars is nothing all that unusual."

"Let's go back to our car. Let's stay there. I'm scared, Alex."

CHAPTER

10

THE ROAD UP THE MOUNTAIN TOOK A BEND, AND AS soon as he was around it Billy Connery suddenly veered his horse into the woods and down into a ravine. He followed it a hundred yards, then dismounted and tethered the horse to some brush. Here it was well out of sight from the road. He gave it oats from the feed bag he'd brought from the livery, then cut a straight path toward the road, not the angled path by which he'd reached this point.

He lay in the brush by the roadside and waited. He was there hardly a minute before the approach of two horsemen confirmed the suspicion that had developed about a mile out of town.

This was the pair he'd seen in the gun shop. He shook his head as he watched them pass. He should have never flashed that roll of money so carelessly.

They rode within fifteen feet of where Connery hid, one of them urging the other to hurry because he feared their prey was moving faster than they were.

Ride on, scoundrels, Connery thought. *You're chasing phantoms now.*

They went on and he debated what to do. They probably would figure out before long that he had evaded them and might turn around. So he didn't want to get back on the road and take the chance of meeting them on the return.

Nothing to do but stay out of sight and wait it out, then. That could mean he'd not make Culvertown tonight.

Well, there could be worse fates. Such as being robbed at gunpoint.

He went back to his horse and removed its saddle. He rubbed the horse down as best he could and fed it some more.

Too bad he didn't have a bedroll. He'd not anticipated needing one unless his search for Kenton took him into the mountains beyond Culvertown. In that case he'd planned to buy what he needed in Culvertown.

He'd spent other nights in harder situations. He'd make do, if it came to it.

Maybe he'd get lucky and his followers would come back sooner rather than later and he could ride on and maybe make Culvertown before nightfall.

Connery returned to his hiding place beside the road to keep a hopeful watch.

He dozed off, though he didn't realize it until sound on the road made him wake up. He looked around, then ducked low as he realized that his followers had indeed given up and reversed course.

Connery kept quiet and grinned. Once they were past, he could saddle up again and head on into Culvertown. He'd get there in the middle of the night, but what the devil? At the worst he'd sleep in a barn loft or woodshed, better than the open woods without a bedroll.

The two riders were moving slowly and drinking.

"Too damn bad he give us the slip," one said.

"Hell, yeah. I never seen such a roll of bills. I can't figure how the hell he got away from us."

"Heard us following, betcha. Heard your damn mouth blabbing on. I told you to be quieter."

"Hell, you was making more noise than me. Hey, why you stopping?"

"Gotta wet."

One of the pair slid out of the saddle and headed straight for the woods, only a few yards from where Connery hid. Connery held still as he listened to liquid splattering the ground. Thank heaven the man wasn't any closer than he was.

There was a loud thump out on the road. The other man had fallen out of his saddle.

The first one headed back out to the road, staggering badly. Connery realized just how drunk this pair was.

"What the hell's the matter with you?" the staggering man said.

The other was trying to pick himself up and not doing a good job of it.

"I'm drunk, Wayne. I fell off my horse."

"Ha! You never could hold your whiskey, Hamp. Get up off that ground."

Hamp tried hard but wound up on his rump again.

"Hell, Wayne, I can't go no farther. We got bedrolls. Let's just lay 'em out and sleep it off here. We'll ride back down in the morning."

Connery winced. If they camped where they were, he was stuck where he was. . . . He dared not move for fear of making noise.

"Come on, Hamp. Get back on your horse. You can make it."

That's right, Hamp, Connery thought. *You can make it.*

"I can't. I can't. Let's stay here and go in come morning."

The debate continued briefly, and in the end Hamp won out. Connery shook his head sadly. An entire night hiding in the brush mere yards away from a couple of drunken thieves! The prospect was miserable.

Maybe they'd pass out and he could sneak off to his horse.

But they didn't pass out. They built a fire right in the midst of the road and sat drinking and talking, their voices growing more slurred. Billy wondered how much they could drink before finally succumbing. Their capacity seemed boundless.

Their conversation was about women, past crimes, and ambitions for future ones that would make them wealthy men. Connery had his doubts about that. These were losers, probably destined to die young and broke and still dreaming of that big crime.

He wished they were dreaming somewhere else to-night.

"Take a look there," Hamp said, pointing in Con-nery's general direction and giving him a scare. But he realized quickly that Hamp was not pointing at him but somewhere beyond him. "You can see the light of Jack Livingston's place from here."

"Nah. That ain't Livingston's place. It's too far away. Besides, I hear the place is empty. Livingston died last year."

"He ain't dead. I've talked to three men who seen him in Culvertown not three months ago. And six months back, he come into town and walked into a saloon and bought three rounds for everybody in the place. Told them to drink up hearty. Then two of them followed him back toward his mansion and dang if he didn't shoot at them. He's loco as can be, Jack Liv-ingston is."

"Loco, maybe, but rich, too. They say that place has gold hid all through it."

"Just a story. Jack Livingston used to be rich, but he ain't no more."

"Who told you that?"

"Bunch of folks. He made a big strike here at Cul-vertown and got rich as Beelzebub and married him-self off to a woman who had to have herself a fancy big mansion. So he built her one, and filled it all full of tunnels and passages and such."

"That's just another wild tale."

"Hell, no, it ain't. . . . I've talked to folks who say

they've seen 'em. His wife liked book stories with big old houses and secret tunnels and such, and so he built her house that way. Then she up and dies on him, and he goes loco and lives up there alone. Except sometimes he goes off here and there and gambles. So he loses most his money, but every now and then wins him a big hand and gets a lot of it back. That's when he shows up in Culvertown, buying drinks and all."

"I don't believe none of that."

"Well, I'm just telling what I hear."

"Tell you what: if there is money or gold hid up in that mansion, I'd sure like to put my hands on it."

"Amen. That would be a place worth robbing. But you'll not catch me trying it."

"Why?"

"Don't you know? Everyone who's tried to rob Jack Livingston ain't come back from the effort."

"Just more stories, that's all."

"The hell! You go into the Livingston mansion, you don't come out again."

They talked longer, dreaming out loud about the wealth they would someday steal. They drank, too, growing drunker and drunker, until finally they did slide into unconsciousness.

By then Billy Connery was asleep as well. He did not waken until the next morning. He awakened abruptly, though, startled into awareness by something . . . but he couldn't quite remember what it was. Popping sounds. That's what it had been. Like pinewood snapping in a fireplace, but louder. Gunshots? Faraway ones, maybe. The pair on the road were gone, their fire nearly cold. He was glad to see the last of them.

He got up, rubbing the back of his stiff neck, and headed off to where his horse awaited.

CHAPTER

11

CONNERY HAD BEEN CLOSER TO CULVERTOWN THAN he had realized. After only a couple of hours of riding he rounded a bend and saw the town spread out before him.

It was a beautiful and clear morning, but that only served to better define the town's remarkable ugliness. It was a rambling, undefined, mostly unpainted, smoke-stained town, streets muddy, boardwalks uneven. All around the town, rude cabins marked the hills, which were lined by a network of footpaths and wagon trails. To the west, a huge water cannon blasted away at the mountainside, laying bare rock and adding abundant filth to the wide stream that flowed through the center of town.

Welcome to Culvertown. Connery shook his head as he rode in, thinking that Brady Kenton couldn't have picked a less appealing place in which to hide.

He yanked his horse to a halt, however, when his eyes fell on one unexpected exception to the rule of ugliness that governed the town.

On a mountainside stood nothing less than a mansion, looming over the town. Connery let out a low whistle. This had to be the Jack Livingston mansion that the two scoundrels on the road had talked about.

Astonishing. Absolutely astonishing.

He found three hotels and picked the best-looking of the three. The man behind the counter was fleshy and bearded but had eyes that were bright and friendly, at least until Connery asked for a room.

"Ain't got none," the man said coldly.

"Your sign outside says you do."

"Well, what do you know? An Irishman who can read."

Connery understood then, debated mentally whether to fight it or just say the devil with it. The latter. He had better things to do with his time than try to overcome the prejudices of some mountain hotel keeper.

He left the hotel and headed for the second-best one. This time he disguised his brogue, just in case, and got a room with no problem and also arranged for the hotel livery boy to take care of his horse.

Baggage in hand, he headed upstairs to his room.

He was on the street again before long, in his hand the envelope bearing the apparent Kenton sketch. Briefly he admired the technical quality again, then glanced at the front to remind himself of the cafe name. The Buckeye. He set out to find it.

In a town this small he didn't expect it to take long, but Culvertown was cluttered and patternless, and he searched for more than an hour before at last he found the place.

The Buckeye was a nicer place than Connery had anticipated. He walked in and found a vacant table in a corner, from which he had a good view of the entire room. Settling there, he looked around for the waiter depicted in the sketch. But he didn't see him.

A different waiter, bald, short, and plump, approached him. "What can I get for you, sir?"

"Coffee. A piece of apple pie if you've got it."

"We've got custard, sir. That's all the pie we have today."

"Custard it is."

When the coffee and pie came to him on a tray, Connery slid the envelope toward the waiter.

"If you would, sir, take a look at that picture. Is that someone you know?"

The waiter picked it up. "I'll be! That's a picture of Walter Wheelan."

"A waiter here?"

"Not anymore, sir."

This was not good news. "Is he gone from town?"

"Not yet. But in a day or so he'll be moving to Chicago. Walter has gotten married, and his wife doesn't much like small mining towns."

"I see."

"May I ask you if you drew that picture, sir?"

"I didn't draw it. In fact, I'm trying to find the man who did. It was drawn in this very cafe."

"It's quite remarkable. . . . It looks exactly like Walter. Even the way he stands."

Connery took a sip of coffee and picked up his fork. "Have you seen anyone in here doing sketches like this?"

"Indeed I haven't, sir."

"Do you think that Walter Wheelan might know who did this sketch?"

"You'd have to ask him, sir."

"Can you tell me where I can find him?"

For a moment the waiter seemed uncertain, maybe a touch suspicious. "Why do you want to know?"

"I think the artist might be someone I know professionally. I'm an illustrator for *Gunnison's Illustrated American*."

"No! I do love to read that magazine. Though I miss Brady Kenton's touch. It's sad that he passed away."

"Yes. But about Walter Wheelan . . ."

"He lives in a rented room above a hardware store one street over. Unless he's moved away already. I've lost contact with him since he quit working here."

"What's the hardware store?"

"Smith's Hardware and Dry Goods."

"Thank you." Connery took his first bite of pie.

The waiter lingered a moment, looking at the sketch again. "I would half-believe that this sketch was done by Brady Kenton himself!"

"It is remarkably good."

"Who is the artist you believe did this sketch?"

"No one you'd have heard of," Connery said, because he could hardly tell the truth without sounding insane.

"I hope you find him, and hire him for your magazine. It would be wonderful to see this kind of work in it again . . . almost like having Kenton back again."

"There's more truth in that statement than you can know."

"Beg your pardon?"

"Never mind. The pie is good."

"Thank you, sir." The waiter turned to walk away, but a stray thought came to Connery's mind, a possibility that had been playing at the edge of his thoughts ever since he'd entered town, and he called the waiter back.

"What can you tell me about that big mansion on the mountainside?"

"Have you not heard of Jack Livingston, sir?"

"Maybe I've heard the name. But I don't know much about him."

"Not many do. . . . There are more rumors than facts."

"I heard he had died."

"Not that I know of, sir. There's someone living up there now. I've seen lights at night."

"Does Livingston have family?"

"His wife died. I think he had a son by a woman he was married to before . . ." The waiter lowered his voice. "Or maybe not really married to, if you know what I mean."

"How long have you been reading the *Illustrated American*?"

The waiter lifted a brow; Connery knew his stream of shifting questions must seem odd. The waiter would think them worthwhile when he received his sizable tip. "A lot of years, sir."

"Do you ever recall Brady Kenton having done a story about Jack Livingston?"

The other frowned, thinking back. "I don't know that I do."

"Really? Because I have the notion that he did. But I'm not sure." He paused and stared into his coffee cup. "If Brady Kenton knew Jack Livingston, then Jack Livingston might be just the kind of man who could help Kenton hide."

"Hide? But he's dead."

"I know. But if he wasn't, and if he wanted to hide, what better place than a place like that?"

The waiter was looking increasingly uncertain about his customer.

"I'll finish my pie now," Connery said, smiling.

"Very good, sir."

When Connery left the cafe, he paused and looked up at the mansion. Just a feeling . . . and a fragment of something that might be a memory.

The more he thought about it, the more sure he felt that Kenton had once done a story about an eccentric rich man who built a mansion for his wife above a Colorado mining town. It had to be Jack Livingston. How many others like him could there be?

Connery would visit the local telegraph office very soon and send a wire back to the *Illustrated American*. A search of the magazine's morgue would quickly answer the question.

For now, though, there was another visit to make. Connery stepped off the boardwalk and set out to find Smith's Hardware and Dry Goods.

CHAPTER

12

As soon as the door to the room above the hardware store opened, Billy Connery lost any possible doubt that the artist who had done the sketch on the envelope was Brady Kenton. The sketch had perfectly captured not only the image but also the very stance and impression of the man who stood before Connery in the open doorway.

"What can I do for you?" Walter Wheelan asked. He was a little rumpled and weary-looking and surrounded by packed crates and boxes. The arm garters he'd worn in the sketch Kenton had done were not present now. The man had been packing up to move.

"My name's Billy Connery," Connery replied, still suppressing his Irish accent, just in case Wheelan was another one of those who found Irishmen intolerable. "I wanted to meet you, just for a few moments, and ask you some questions about something."

"What kind of questions?"

"Nothing to worry about. Just some personal business I'm conducting. Congratulations on your marriage, by the way."

"Who told you about that?"

"A waiter at the Buckeye. One of your former co-workers."

"What's this all about?"

"Just this." Connery produced the envelope and showed it to Wheelan.

"I'll be!" Wheelan said, looking at the image of himself. "Where'd you get that? Did you draw that?"

"No. It was found in the Buckeye. Not by me, but someone who was there a while back, and who lent it to me. You haven't seen it before?"

"No. Who drew it?"

"That's the question I'm trying to answer. I'm a professional illustrator, and I'd like to find the one who did this. He's quite good, as you can see. Excellent."

"I'd say so. Looks just like me."

"You never noticed a customer sketching you at one time or another in the last few weeks?"

Wheelan thought a few moments. "Well, maybe I did, though I didn't know he was drawing. There was a man with a pencil . . . I thought he was writing."

This didn't necessarily mean anything. Any number of people probably jotted down notes or wrote letters in cafes. But just in case, Connery pressed on. "Do you recall what he looked like?"

"Not really. I think he was a fairly tall fellow. Beard. That's about all."

Maybe they were getting somewhere after all. "How old?"

"Lord, I don't remember. Not young, not old. Just a man."

"Tell me: have you ever seen this man before?" Connery pulled from under his vest a page torn from a magazine. He unfolded it and handed it to Wheelan.

"I've seen this picture," Wheelan said. "This is the picture of Brady Kenton that always ran in the *Illustrated American,* before he died."

"I need to ask you a question that may seem odd. Did the man you saw with the pencil in the café look like Brady Kenton?"

Wheelan laughed. "What kind of joke is this? Brady Kenton's dead!"

"I know. But the man you saw . . . did he look like Kenton?"

"I guess he could have looked like him. But a lot of people could. Kenton is dead. You're not trying to say he isn't, are you? Because . . . hey! Hey, you there! Get out of there!"

Wheelan's attention had suddenly been diverted by someone behind Connery. Connery turned and saw a boy of about ten come running out of a half-opened door of an apartment across from Wheelan's room. The boy darted within a yard of Connery and down the stairs. He had something in his hands—a loaf of bread, Connery thought it was.

"Damned little scoundrel!" Wheelan said. "Sorry thief! You leave a door unlocked around here and that little devil will be through it, taking whatever he can.

I've caught him in here before! It taught me to keep my door locked, I'll tell you."

"So he doesn't live in those rooms?"

"Hell, no!"

"It looked like he'd taken bread."

"He lives on what he can steal half the time. I suppose I should feel sorry for him."

"If he's hungry enough to steal bread, I think there's no choice but to feel sorry for him. Is he an orphan?"

"He'd be better off if he was. He's got no mother, but his father's still alive. But the sorry old devil drinks bad, and beats the boy so bad he has to spend a lot of his time in hiding. I really do suppose I should feel more sorry for him than I do. I just can't abide a thief under any circumstance, that's all. The people who live across the hall there have given that boy food, money, clothes, time and time again. And here he goes stealing from them!"

Connery found this all dismaying and depressing. He'd spent enough time here. Taking back the picture of Kenton, he thanked Wheelan again and turned away.

"Hey, you really weren't trying to say that Kenton is still alive, were you?"

Connery turned and looked at Wheelan a last time. "Why? Do you think he could be?"

"Not if what I read in your magazine is true. He was killed along the railroad near Denver."

"Then I guess you answered your own question. Good day to you, Mr. Wheelan."

"Good day to you, sir. I hope you find your mysterious sketch artist."

"I intend to, sir."

Connery moved on, but Wheelan called to him one more time. "Hey, I think I just remembered something. That man writing with the pencil came back in later on. He looked around the table he'd been at, but wouldn't stay to eat. I remember because I tried to seat him and he wouldn't sit down."

"He was looking for this sketch, then."

"Assuming that man was the one who did it. It could have been somebody else. Like I said, I just figured the man was writing down notes or something. I didn't really specifically notice him drawing."

Connery thought it all over as he walked slowly through town, looking for the telegraph office. If it had been Kenton that Wheelan saw laboring with a pencil and paper and if Kenton had returned to seek the envelope he'd left, then he must have been concerned that the envelope drawing would be found and serve to identify him.

As fate would have it, that very thing had occurred.

Connery found the telegraph office and sent a wire to the *Illustrated American*. After an hour of waiting the reply came back. Kenton had indeed done a story and series of sketches about Jack Livingston.

Connery tucked the telegram into his pocket, beside the envelope bearing the sketch. He was now almost sure why Kenton had come to this unlikely town. He needed a remote, secure place to hide. And what more remote and secure place could there be than the mountainside mansion of Jack Livingston?

Connery walked out of the telegraph office into the midst of excitement in Culvertown: a crowd was gathering around a town marshal who was bringing in two dead bodies draped without dignity across the back of a mule, their arms dangling.

"What happened, Marshal?" someone asked.

"Shot dead," he replied. "Both of them. A traveler coming in early this morning found them on the road, both shot square between the eyes."

"Between the eyes?" someone replied. "Executed?"

"No powder burns on the face," the marshal replied. "Whoever shot them plugged them from some distance away . . . some really accurate shooting, to hit them both like he did." He touched his face directly between the eyebrows. "Hell of a time for it to happen, though. I've got a train to catch to Scallonville this afternoon, and now I've got to deal with this. I'll be lucky to make it on time."

Connery was feeling a little queasy. The men on the back of the mule were the same ones who had followed him and camped on the road the night before.

He remembered the popping sounds that had awakened him. Now he knew what those sounds had been.

He listened to the general conversation around him. Someone noted that the two were a pair of common thieves who had plagued people in those parts for at least a year. Whoever had killed them had done the citizenry a favor, another person noted.

Connery stared for a few moments at the blood dripping from the downturned heads of the dead men and listened to the talk around him. He was a little shaky. Though these men had been a threat to him and he certainly had no trace of affection for them, it was unnerving to see them dead when only last night he'd been hiding from them along the roadside.

He turned away from the crowd and walked off, feeling the need for a change of scenery and a turn around town for some fresh air.

Connery walked briskly, not noticing that another man had also stepped away from the crowd and was following him some distance behind.

CHAPTER

13

"HEY, YOU, MISTER!"

Connery turned. The little bread-stealing boy he'd seen earlier was approaching him. He wore a cocky grin and had a hardened and mature aura about him that belied his years. The face was that of a boy, the glint of the eyes that of a man.

The boy marched up to Connery and thrust his hand out, a gesture that surprised Connery. But he took the offered hand and the boy pumped it firmly.

"You need to be a little more careful, mister," the boy said. "You dropped something back there on the street."

He handed Connery both the return telegram he'd just received minutes before from the *Illustrated American* and the envelope bearing the sketch of Walter Wheelan.

Connery was surprised. Both of these items had been thrust deep into his coat pocket . . . hadn't they? He'd had his hands in his pockets back there while examining the dead men and supposed he could have accidentally dragged these items out when he withdrew his hands from his pockets.

Then again, this little scamp might have picked his pockets while he was distracted. He'd be willing to bet a boy like this had that kind of talent. Well, at least he'd given them back. And a quick feel of Connery's pockets revealed his wallet was still in place.

"Thank you," he said.

"I know that man in the picture," the boy announced. "That's Walter Wheelan."

"That's right. In fact, I was talking to him this morning when you came out of those boarding rooms and he shouted at you. Remember seeing me there?"

"I remember. I remember what you two was talking about, too."

"You listened to our conversation?"

"I listen to every conversation I can. You can learn a lot worth the hell knowing if you just listen to folks."

Cocky, sharp-tongued little street boy, Connery thought. But the thought bore no edge. Connery had been a sharp-tongued street boy himself some years earlier.

"What's your name?"

"I'm Stockton Shelley." The hand came up again for another shake, which Connery found slightly amusing. "Pleased to know you, Mr. Connery."

"I'm impressed. You even know my name."

"I heard you tell it to Walter Wheelan. You came up to his door at just the wrong time, you know. I was just about to sneak out when you came up and brought him to his door. I couldn't sneak out then."

"So why did you make a break for it?"

"Because I looked out the window and saw the man whose apartment I was in coming back home. I had to get out before he got in."

"It's not right to steal, you know."

"It was just a loaf of bread. And Walter Wheelan has stole enough food from the Buckeye during the time he worked there that I'll be damned if I care what he thinks about me getting some food for myself. A man's got to eat, after all."

"Are you hungry?"

"Not no more. I ate a whole loaf of bread. Hey, will you give me some money for bringing you back them papers?"

"To tell you the truth, it'd crossed my mind that maybe I didn't drop those papers at all."

"What? You saying I stole them?"

"If you'll steal bread, you'll pick pockets."

"You're hurting my feelings, mister!"

"Yeah, I imagine you're quite a sensitive young man. But I tell you what: I will give you some money. Not for picking my pockets, but because I'm just a very nice fellow."

Stockton accepted the coin gratefully. After biting it, he bowed to Connery and said, "You're a gentleman and a scholar, sir! A gentleman and a scholar!"

"Kind of you to say so. Good day to you, young man."

"Hold up there, Mr. Irishman. I think you'll be paying me a bit more than this."

"What? Are you going to rob me now?"

"Oh, no. You're going to want to pay me for what I've got to tell you."

"And what might that be?"

"It's who did this drawing of old Wheelan, that's what."

"It may surprise you to learn that I'm already fairly certain who did it. The question is, where can I find him?"

"Maybe I can tell you both things."

"I'm looking for more than maybes."

"I know for a fact who it is, and where he is."

Connery pulled five dollars from his pocket and handed it to Stockton. "Five more if what you tell me proves to be right."

The boy took the money smugly, pinching it between thumb and forefinger and lifting it from Connery's hand. "The man who drew that picture is Brady Kenton. Folks say he's dead, but he ain't, because I've seen him. He combs his hair different than in that picture of him in the magazine, and he's got a longer beard. But it's him."

"All right. You've told me what I already knew. Where is he?"

The boy pointed in the direction of the Jack Livingston mansion.

Connery nodded. "Somehow I had the feeling that might be the place."

"He may as well be on the moon, though, if you want to see him," Stockton said. "Old Livingston ain't going to let you in. He don't let anybody in much."

"He apparently let in Brady Kenton. Or do you really know Kenton is there?"

"I do know. I've seen him."

"Where?"

"Sitting on a rain barrel out behind the saloon, drawing on a busted-off piece of a wooden crate. Then he got up and walked on up to the Livingston house."

Connery frowned. "Was he drinking out behind that saloon?"

"Had him a bottle. I saw him take a swallow or two."

Gunnison would not be glad to learn this. But it was not unexpected, given Kenton's history.

"Was there a woman with him?"

"No. He was alone. Where's the rest of my money?"

"You'll get it when I've met Kenton face-to-face. I have to verify that what you've told me is true." Stockton frowned, chewed on his lip, then said, "If I can bring Kenton to you will you make that other five into twenty-five?"

"Why should I pay you when I can go up and knock on Livingston's door myself?"

"Livingston don't answer his door . . . except with a shotgun, or a pack of biting dogs."

Connery found himself irritated by this manipulative, self-serving boy, even if he did sympathize for his poor situation in life. Stockton had probably overheard enough during the conversation with Wheelan to figure out what he needed to say to gouge money out of Connery.

"I'll take my chances. If I can't get to Kenton, then maybe I'll look you up."

Stockton pocketed his money. "I'll be seeing you later, then."

When Stockton Shelley had gone out of sight, sauntering and swaggering like a miniature gunfighter, Connery looked up at the Livingston mansion and wondered if it really would be as challenging to get to Kenton as had been implied. And what if Livingston was a true lunatic, and dangerous?

Connery stood staring up at the Livingston house, trying to decide exactly what he would say when he got there.

CHAPTER

14

O<small>N THE OTHER SIDE OF A WHITE LINEN CURTAIN</small>
that hung over most of one of the upper windows in
the Livingston mansion, Brady Kenton gazed down at
the lone figure of Billy Connery.

Kenton had not met Connery and had no inkling
of who he was looking at. It was not unusual, though,
to see someone down below staring up at the house.
It was, after all, quite an impressive structure, not typical of mountain mining towns. Long after Jack Livingston was dead and gone, Kenton figured, some
canny community leader type would probably per-
suade the town leaders to make Livingston's house
into some sort of museum or historical attraction. Ex-
isting legends of the solitary eccentric would be en-
hanced and new ones created. Livingston would
become the fictionalized symbol of a Culvertown of
years past.

But probably not much fictionalized. Livingston
was enough of a true eccentric not to require much
exaggeration. He was a rough man, a hard man, a man

easy to come to hate . . . and sometimes a part of Kenton still did, despite himself.

But thank God Livingston was here. Thank God he'd allowed his fortress of a mansion to become a refuge at a time Kenton had never needed a refuge more.

While Kenton watched, the gazing man in the town below reached into a pocket and pulled out a pad. Producing a pencil, he began to write . . . no, to draw. Kenton was startled: it was like watching a reflection of himself at work.

Could the man below be an illustrator, just as Kenton was? If so, why was he here, now, drawing this particular dwelling?

Kenton had cause to be unnerved by this. He stepped away from the window.

The room suddenly made him feel claustrophobic. He went out, into the hall, then down two more doors.

He rapped lightly. "Come in," a soft voice on the other side replied.

Kenton opened the door and entered slowly. He closed the door behind him and smiled at a woman the sight of whom still made his heart hammer like a drum, though they'd now been together for many weeks.

Victoria Kenton smiled back at her husband and lifted her hand, bidding him to come.

Kenton walked across to her and knelt. She was in a wicker chair, a quilt across her legs, and though she looked weak and thin, she was yet beautiful.

He was ever amazed, in fact, that years and the

trials of injury and illness that this woman had suffered had not robbed her of more beauty than they had. Though she was in her fifties now and her hair abundantly touched with gray, her face was still the beautiful vision that Kenton had secretly buried in almost every illustration he had drawn . . . looking out a window, around a corner, sometimes actually embodied in the drawn lines and shadows of trees, buildings, mountains.

She was still his Victoria, and after so many long years of separation, she was his again.

"Did you rest?" he asked, holding her hand as he knelt beside her chair.

"I did. I slept right here in this chair. I feel stronger now."

"I think your color is better. I wish you'd slept longer. Maybe if you'd lie down on the bed . . ." He glanced at the four-poster on the other side of the large room. Victoria's bed, the bed he longed to share with her but which, for now, remained hers alone. They had been separated for too many years for her to welcome him instantly back into her bed. It would take time. They still had to come to know each other again. But it would happen. Every day Brady Kenton felt that Victoria was a little more his again; that little bit of the life and closeness they had lost had come back again.

"The chair is comfortable enough for me. Back in England I spent most of my time in a chair. It was the dream that woke me."

Dear heaven, how good it was to hear her voice!

Kenton drank in the melody of it like a perfect wine. "A good dream, I hope."

"No. It wasn't. I dreamed he found us. I dreamed that he shot you."

"Victoria . . . don't dwell on such things. It's only your fear speaking. He's not going to find us, not this far away. We're a world away from him now."

"No, Brady. You don't know him like I do. He will never abide that you took me away from him. He'll search for us forever, until he finds us."

"He'll not find us here, Victoria. I can think of no safer place for you."

She stroked Kenton's face. "Oh, Brady . . . you're so courageous and devoted and reassuring . . . but if only you knew David like I do! You would understand that in his own way, he is as devoted to me as you are. He loves me, just as you do . . . but his love isn't the love of a normal man. He only knows how to love by possessing and controlling, and he can't stand to lose. And he will especially not stand to lose me. He would rather kill me than lose me."

"He will never kill you. I'll not allow it. I'd die myself before I'd let him near you."

She smiled, a sad smile. "Let me tell you what he will do, what I have no doubt he has already done," she said. "He will not remain in England. He'll follow us here."

"Nonsense, dear. Please don't worry about—"

"Listen to me, Brady! I speak as one who has known this man for many years. He will follow us to the United States. Once here, he'll use his money freely, hiring the best investigators and the toughest hired gunmen he can to find our track. He will discover, eventually if not already, that I have a half brother, and that his name is Livingston, and that he lives in Culvertown, Colorado, in a strong but remote and seldom-visited mansion. He'll consider that it may be a place we would come to take refuge . . . because he knows that I know he will come after us."

CHAPTER

15

THOUGH HIS HUSBAND'S INSTINCTS MADE KENTON want to tell Victoria that all this was nonsense and all was well, he knew she was right. Of course Dr. David Kevington would come after them! Kenton had known it all along. It was why they had come here, to this obscure, high mountain town, to take up hiding in the house of Jack Livingston, a place Kenton hoped that Dr. Kevington would never find.

Victoria went on. "He'll work as long as he has to, and spend as much as he has to, to make sure we are found. He'll send men to kill you and to take me back to him . . . or maybe he'll kill me as well, to punish me for having gone away with you."

"Don't talk about such things, my dear."

"I have to. Because we have to face this, Brady. Our lives can never be normal lives until the matter of David Kevington has been dealt with. He stalked after me like a wild beast all those years ago and kidnapped me all the way to England and hid me away like his private treasure all these years, telling me you were dead and gone and that only he loved me . . . that he was my husband. He took away the child I bore to you, Brady, and gave her to a servant. He is an evil and desperate man. He *will not* let us be! Deny it if you will, but I know that you believe I'm right. If you didn't believe it, you would have been in contact by now with your magazine, your partner, your friends. You know you dare not go to them because you know that if you do, you might bring danger upon them."

Kenton could not dispute this. He nodded, heavy of heart.

Victoria, not used to much speaking, was growing weary. Despite the years that had passed since the railroad accident that had been the watershed event of both her own and Brady Kenton's lives, she was still an injured woman. She had spent years in a comatose to semicomatose condition, even given birth to a daughter without knowing it. Victoria's injuries had left her brain injured and her mind weakened along with her body. But she was stronger now, her mind focused and clear most of the time, the lies that her obsessed kidnapper had told her now seen for what they were.

There were periods, though, when her mind would grow cloudy. She would push Kenton away at those times, refusing to see him. Three times he had been so disheartened by her rejections that he had left the house and gone into Culvertown, where he would drink and sulk and work on idle and pointless sketches. It was foolish, he knew, because he ran the risk of being identified. He worried still about one sketch of a waiter he'd scribbled down for no good reason on an envelope at a local cafe. He'd left the sketch behind by accident and now worried that some-one might recognize it as a Brady Kenton work.

But it wasn't likely, he told himself. All America believed Brady Kenton to be dead.

"We can't hide here for long, Brady. He'll come, or he'll send men to deal with us. And it isn't fair to Jack. He's endangered as well, as long as we're here."

Kenton struggled against the sense of despair that so often threatened to overwhelm him these days. He'd not expected despair to be one of the emotions that would remain with him after reuniting with the wife he had loved and missed for so long.

"I don't think Jack worries about any kind of dan-ger," Kenton said, trying to sound brighter than he felt. "Jack rather likes a challenge, I think. He'd prob-ably tell David Kevington to send in his little army, then laugh while he picked them all off through those rifle ports he's built into the walls here."

"Don't take what I say lightly, Brady. We must leave soon, or Jack may pay the price."

In his current state of mind, Kenton might have barked back that he hardly cared about any price Jack Livingston might pay. In his younger days, Livingston had treated his half sister, Victoria, very badly, cheat-ing her out of an inheritance that should have been hers. Victoria had not cared much about the material loss, but the fact that her half brother had taken such advantage of her had hurt her so badly that she'd virtually disavowed his existence. Kenton himself had held a long grudge against Jack Livingston, though a few years back, in a time of personal reflection, he'd chosen to visit Jack and heal over the old wounds. At the same time, Kenton had written and illustrated a well-received story about his eccentric half brother-in-law and made Livingston a relatively famous figure.

Even though the rift had ostensibly been repaired between Kenton and Jack Livingston, ghosts of the old ill feelings remained, and Kenton still believed that Livingston owed Victoria some recompense for the way he'd mistreated her years before.

Maybe, Kenton thought, *he's giving that recompense by allowing us to hide here. I'll try not hold ill will against him. Right now he may be saving our lives.*

"We will leave, then . . . when we can. But your health won't allow it yet, Victoria. Our flight from England, the stress of travel all the way across the country, all our various worries . . . they've left you too weak for us to do anything but stay here for now. Besides, I've seen no indications at all that anyone has followed us." He suddenly thought of the man he'd seen outside, sketching the mansion, and wondered . . . but then he dismissed it. Anyone sent by Dr. Kevington would be up to more nefarious stuff than standing in the open, sketching a mansion.

"I'll be able to travel soon. I don't want to be a danger to anyone."

Kenton leaned over and kissed her cheek, thanking

God deeply that she was alive and here to be kissed at all. He'd lived in a world that for year upon year had told him his wife was dead. Only he had stubbornly refused to accept that "fact," and he had been proven correct.

"We'll find another place," Kenton said. "I know people all over this nation who will be glad to help us."

The truth was, at the moment he couldn't think of anywhere else to go at all.

CHAPTER

16

THE DOOR OPENED. NO KNOCK OR FOREWARNING.

Jack Livingston appeared. He was on the short side but muscular, with silver-gray hair trimmed close to his head and a weathered face with intense dark gray eyes.

"Well, Victoria, how are you feeling?"

"I'm doing quite well, Jack," she said, not quite truthfully. She was beginning to pave the way toward their exit from this place. "I had a good nap."

Jack walked over to them. By now Kenton had come to his feet. Jack gazed down at his half sister. "I still can't believe you're here, Victoria. Can't believe you're alive. All them years that old Brady here spent looking for you, I thought he was crazy. So did a lot of others."

Kenton smiled just a little. "I might note that there are plenty who think you're a little crazy yourself, Jack. You live up here in this big house, run people off who come around, act like a hermit . . . then every now and then you take a notion to go to town and buy everybody a drink."

"It ain't always that. Once I went into the Buckeye and bought everybody in the place a plate of flapjacks."

"You're an odd man, Jack. Then again, so am I, I suppose."

Jack smiled at his half sister. "Your face is as pretty as ever, Victoria, but I can see the tracks of what you've been through in your eyes. What did this Kevington fellow do to you?"

"He loved me, and he imprisoned me. He saved my life, then took my life away. He delivered my daughter while I lay unconscious, then gave her to a servant family to raise as their own. He declared that I would have all the good things life could offer, but denied me my freedom. He told me I was his wife, but treated me as his slave. In short, he subjected me to a life of contradictions, Jack. That was my life with Dr. David Kevington."

Livingston's left cheek twitched. "I'd like to shoot the bastard myself."

"I'd like to beat you to it," Kenton said. "I almost had the opportunity, you know."

"Did you? I wish you'd done it. Was that while you were spiriting Victoria out of his estate?"

"Yes. I'll tell you all about it sometime."

"Now's as good a time as any, seems to me."

"Later, maybe." Kenton wasn't about to go into details on the spot of what had been a horrifying series of events for Victoria. His removal of her from the Kevington estate near London had been nearly fatal for both of them. When Kenton thought back on the rabid fury that Kevington had displayed when he caught Kenton smuggling away the woman he had in his snare for years, it was easy to realize that Victoria was right when she predicted that Kevington would surely come after them.

"There's things about this I have a right to know," Jack said. "Is Kevington likely to show up here?"

"I don't believe Kevington is likely to find us easily . . . but eventually, yes, I think he will find us. We were just talking about that, Victoria and I, when you came in." Kenton didn't figure this was news to Livingston, who probably had been crouched with his ear to keyhole throughout the couple's conversation.

Kenton despised having to live under the protection of a man he never would really like.

"Let him come," Livingston said icily. "I'll blow his candle out for him."

Kenton realized that Victoria had grown tense in the last few moments, her knuckles whitening as she gripped the armrest of the wicker chair. He felt a surge of mixed emotions. As much as he didn't like to admit it, he knew Victoria still held an affection of a sort for Kevington—who had, after all, nursed her away from the brink of death after her train accident. It was probably difficult for her to listen to him and Livingston talking about killing Kevington as if it would be a privilege.

Victoria had made it clear that she hated Kevington, but Kenton knew that her hatred was not pure.

For her there would always be a measure of affection mixed with her loathing. Kenton could not blame her for this. It was possible, maybe likely, that if not for Kevington's intervention after Victoria's railroad accident many years before she might not be alive.

"Come to think of it, maybe it's time to tell you the full story after all, Jack," Kenton said. "Let's go downstairs, leave Victoria in peace, and get ourselves a glass of that good whiskey of yours. Then we'll talk."

Billy Connery had given up sketching the Livingston mansion only minutes after he started. He wasn't in Culvertown to sketch but to find Brady Kenton . . . and now that he had a likely idea of where Kenton was, his courage was failing him.

Part of it was simple fear over how the eccentric Livingston would react to a visitor at his door. But Connery was almost as worried about how Kenton would receive him. The man wasn't hiding for no reason and surely would not be happy to be ferreted out.

So Connery found himself unable just yet to force himself up to that big house on the hill.

A beer was what he needed. Maybe two. A couple of beers, and he'd have the courage to do what needed doing.

He headed for the nearest saloon and along the way chanced to pass the local undertaking parlor. The door opened as he passed; a man came out. Connery looked through the door before it could swing shut and was just at the right angle to see through a second, interior doorway, back into the rear room where the dirty work of undertaking was done.

For just a moment he caught a glimpse of two bodies laid out, one on a slab, naked, the undertaker leaning over it, hard at work, with a cigar dropping hot ashes on the dead man. The other corpse was still clothed and waiting his turn on the floor. The outer door swung closed, and the vision of mortality was gone.

But Connery was shaken. Maybe he'd have three beers instead of two.

In the saloon with the first beer in hand, he further pondered the two dead highwaymen. Who had killed them? Whoever he was, he was a good shot to have plugged both so neatly, from a distance, with shots between the eyes. That was one man the pair shouldn't have tried to rob.

He wondered if the local law would spend much time investigating the deaths. He would be willing to wager that they would not. No one would be much inclined to punish men who had rid the region of two troublesome highwaymen.

So here's to you, whoever you are, he said mentally as he raised his glass to the unknown marksman. *May you forever eliminate thieves and keep our roadways safe . . . and, just in case, may you forever keep your distance from me.*

CHAPTER

17

HIS NAME WAS BAILEY MCCURDEN, AND HE SAT IN a dark corner of the saloon, nursing a beer and watching Billy Connery.

At least, he was relatively sure it was Billy Connery he was watching. The young man across the room didn't look quite the same as Connery's meager little picture in the rear section of the *Illustrated American*. This fellow looked a bit leaner and had hair a touch longer, and the feeble mustache sported by the young man in the magazine illustration was absent from this fellow.

Despite the differences, the more McCurden studied the young man, the more sure he was that it was Connery. The resemblances outweighed the differences. With any luck, young Connery would lead him straight to the man he really wanted to find.

The English physician who had hired him would be pleased. McCurden was on the verge of finding Brady Kenton. He could all but smell it.

It had been fairly easy so far. After being hired by

one Dr. David Kevington in a very covert manner,
McCurden had traveled to St. Louis with several other
hired Kevington operatives to keep an eye on the offices and employees of the *Illustrated American*. A
talk to a low-level staff member who was smoking
his pipe on the doorstep had uncovered the news that
one Billy Connery, an illustrator who was a relatively
recent hire of the magazine, was making sudden preparations to travel, apparently at the behest of Kenton's
old partner, Alex Gunnison. And Connery was saying
very little about the details—just enough to let his
coworkers know that he was on to something very
important.

Sensing a possible lead, McCurden had found Connery's apartment, but without Connery present at the
time. But he had found Connery's neighbor, a baker
named J. R. Randwick, who had proven to be a rich
source of information once plied with a few beers.
Connery was going to Culvertown, Colorado, on some
secretive venture that would involve "bringing a certain somebody back from the dead."

It was easy to figure out from there: Kenton was
in Culvertown, and Connery was being sent to find
him.

McCurden made the same journey only a day after
Connery. He'd traveled quickly after disembarking
the train and would have had a completely unimpeded
journey if not for those two troublesome fools who
had tried to rob him on the road.

They'd been only an annoyance, a momentary
problem. Two quick shots, two slugs between the

eyes, and they were out of consideration.

McCurden continued to sip his beer and watch Connery. The young fellow seemed nervous, McCurden thought. Interesting. Nerves implied that he was on to something important.

Maybe Connery had found Kenton. And where Kenton was, there would be the woman Kevington wanted back.

A very valuable woman. Kevington had made that clear, and McCurden hadn't been able to keep his mind off it ever since. *A very valuable woman.*

He'd not let Connery notice him, if he could help it. But he'd also not let him slip out of his sight.

Connery finished his three beers and stared at the empty mug. He felt a little fuzzy but not any more courageous.

Devil with it. It was time to do what he'd come to do. What was there to knocking on a door, after all? If Livingston wasn't hospitable, it wouldn't be the first door slammed in his face.

But Connery had made one slight shift in his plans while drinking his beers. So instead of heading up the hill toward the Livingston mansion, he headed for the telegraph office.

Unnoticed by Connery, a man in the corner of the cafe also rose and left, scooping up a stray newspaper from a table as he did so.

Before they'd gone in their opposite directions, Gunnison and Connery had made communication arrangements. Telegrams would be worded in such a way as to be clear to their intended recipients but not to others who might read them. Brady Kenton, for example, was to be referred to by initials only, but reversed: "KB." And because it was impossible for Gunnison and Connery to know exactly where each other were at any given moment, telegrams were to be sent to several predesignated stations, which would be checked regularly.

Connery rang the bell on the counter of the telegraph station and waited for the operator, a red-haired man with a wide, pale face and many lingering boyhood freckles. This was a different operator from the man who had been here when Connery telegraphed the *Illustrated American* morgue earlier.

"My name is Billy Connery. Have I by chance received any messages?"

"Let me check." He shuffled papers. "No, nothing."

"All right. I want to send some messages of my own. Five of them, all the same, all to different stations in New York."

"Five different recipients?"

"All to the same person, Alexander Gunnison. Just five different stations."

"Odd arrangement. What's the message?"

" 'KB found in Culvertown. Livingston house. Please come.' Sign it off with 'Connery.' That'll be sufficient."

"All righty."

While the operator clicked out the message, Connery paced around the room, humming nervously, glancing out the windows, tapping his heels on the floors. The door leading out to the station porch stood ajar.

There was no one else in the station besides Connery and the key operator. There was, however, a man on the porch, seated by the open door, reading a newspaper. Connery didn't even notice him until he meandered over to the door and happened to look out, and was slightly startled because he knew no one had been on the porch when he entered only two or three minutes earlier.

The man glanced up. Connery said, "Good day, sir," and withdrew back inside.

"That all you need?" the operator asked.

"That's all. I may get a reply to that. I'll check back in with you to see."

"I'll be here."

Connery stepped out onto the porch, walking past the seated man without a glance. He trotted down the steps and onto the dirt street and wondered if he'd just done the right thing. He'd just sent Alex Gunnison a message that would bring him straight to Culvertown . . . and the honest truth was that Connery really didn't know for sure that Kenton was here. He'd yet to verify anything with his own eyes.

But he'd decided over his beers to go ahead and send the message prematurely. By doing so he preempted a difficult situation for himself later on. If he did find Brady Kenton, Kenton might urge him not to contact Gunnison at all. And Connery frankly didn't want to be put into a situation in which he had to choose his duties. Now the issue was predecided. The message was already sent.

The worst that could happen now was that he'd not find Kenton after all and Gunnison would come racing to Colorado all for nothing.

Maybe if Kenton proved not to be here, he'd be able to get a new wire sent out soon enough to counteract the last one. He told himself he'd done the right thing.

Now there were no more excuses. No more beers to be consumed, no more wires to be sent.

Time to go up the hill and do what needed to be done.

CHAPTER

18

"BEG YOUR PARDON, SIR."

Connery turned. The man who'd been reading the newspaper was behind him, smiling in that uncertain way of those who are approaching strangers. It was just the kind of smile Connery would probably have on his face when the door swung open at the Livingston mansion.

"Well, hello. What can I do for you, sir?"

The man laughed, almost a giggle. "You'll have to pardon me, sir, but I was sitting back on the porch at the telegraph office, and I swear I think I heard you say your name is Billy Connery."

"That's right."

"Oh! Oh, my! Well . . . that's something. It is indeed. I wasn't trying to eavesdrop, you understand. It's just that the door was open, and—"

"That's all right. Do I know you, sir?"

"Oh, no. No. But I think I know you. My name is Jim, Jim Grant. And I'm quite a reader, you see, and my favorite reading has always been *Gunnison's Il-*

lustrated American. Me and a million other people, huh? And I have to ask you if you might just happen to be the Billy Connery who works for the *Illustrated American.* And if you're not, I'm going to be as embarrassed as a man can be." The nervous giggle again.

Connery was astonished. Never before had he been recognized by anyone. Among the journalistic stars of the *Illustrated American,* he shone the dimmest.

"I am with the *Illustrated American,* yes." Now it was Connery who wore a silly grin.

"Oh, my. My goodness. I thought it was you. When I heard your name, and heard you say the name of Alex Gunnison, I thought that it really might be you. Oh, my! This is exciting. You're a talented man, Mr. Connery. I've admired your work."

"I'm surprised you've even noticed it."

"Well, I'll tell you, sir—"

"Please, call me Billy."

"Billy, yes. I'll tell you, Billy, I'm not the average reader. When I get interested in something, or someone, I *really* get interested. A bit of a fanatic about things, I'm afraid. Get a little obsessed."

"I see. I'm flattered that you like my work."

"You know, I think I like your work better than Alex Gunnison's. I wouldn't want you to tell him that, though. Was that *the* Alex Gunnison you were sending a wire to?"

"That was the one."

"Oh, my. That's something! Alex Gunnison. I never got the chance to meet him. But I did meet my hero, the greatest one of all. . . ."

"Brady Kenton?"

"Yes. He even signed a copy of the magazine for me. I have it in a frame now."

"When did you see him?"

"It was five years ago, in Chicago."

"Oh."

"I was so sorry to hear when he died." The man paused, licking his lips and frowning strangely. "I . . . I didn't want to say this . . . it sounds very foolish . . . but do you know that I think I've seen Brady Kenton . . . *since* he died? How's that for strange?" The giggle was even more nervous-sounding this time.

"Wait. . . . When did you see him?"

"Well, day before yesterday."

"Up there?" Connery pointed toward the Livingston mansion.

"No, no, not there. In a boardinghouse dining room, across town. I'd gone in to see if they had a room for my brother, who's coming to visit week after next, and there he was, sitting at the table and eating. He looked a little different, and I had the impression he didn't want to be recognized. But I swear it was him! Though I know it couldn't be, because he's dead."

"Can you show me this boardinghouse?"

"Surely . . . but why?"

"I don't want to say just now. Do you mind showing me the way?"

The man grinned widely. "It would be an honor!"

"Thank you, Mr. Grant."

"Please call me Jim." He stuck out his hand for Connery to shake.

And when he did so, his leather coat gapped open a little and Connery saw that he wore a gun belt. Surprised him; Grant just didn't seem the kind to be carrying a hidden weapon. But Connery himself had a pistol, and he probably wouldn't seem the kind to go armed, either. He dismissed the half-second of caution about going off with this stranger.

"What do you do for a living, Jim?" Connery asked as they walked off together.

"I'm a baker," Grant replied. "Here, turn into this alley."

The alley was narrow and shadowed. "What is this, some kind of shortcut?" Connery asked.

"That's right, a shortcut."

They went into the alley.

"A baker, you say. I've got a friend back in St. Louis who's a baker."

"Oh, yes. J. R. Randwick. I met him."

Connery, who was just ahead of Grant, stopped and turned. "You met J. R.?"

"That's right. But he didn't know me as Jim Grant. I told him my real name. McCurden."

"Who the devil are you?" Connery asked, reaching under his jacket for the shoulder-holstered pistol.

McCurden was ahead of him, though. His own pistol came out much more quickly, and he slammed Connery hard on the temple.

Connery collapsed, stunned but not unconscious. McCurden knelt and quickly removed Connery's pistol from its holster and stuck it under his belt.

"Who am I, you ask? Well, starting right now, I'm you. I'm Mr. Billy Connery. Because you're no longer going to be around to play that role in the little stage play we call life. I'm honored to be your understudy. You've never met Kenton, have you? You were hired after his supposed death. Which means Kenton doesn't really know you." He clicked back the hammer of his pistol and aimed it at Connery's forehead.

But he didn't fire. He frowned and shook his head. "Nah. Too loud. We'll do it quietly."

He put away the pistol and pulled out a long-bladed folding knife. It opened with a click and locked into place.

Connery's consciousness faded as the knife went up. He was oblivious to it altogether when it descended swiftly toward his chest.

The telegraph operator was dozing in a chair leaned back against the wall when McCurden entered the station.

"Up at attention, Red!" McCurden bellowed, startling the moon faced operator out of his chair so fast he knocked it over. "Got a message to send."

The operator ran a hand through his hair and tried to regather his dignity. He picked up the chair, dropped it, picked it up again.

"Yes, sir. A message." He sat down at the key. "What is the name of the recipient?"

"Kevington. Dr. David Kevington. He's in St. Louis at the moment." McCurden grinned. "But when he gets this wire, I can assure you, he'll cut a fast trail to dear old Culvertown."

The operator had no notion of what any of this meant. He picked up his pad of paper and a pencil.

"You can dictate your message now, sir."

The message, broken down into pulses of electricity, made its way across the wires to its destination in St. Louis.

Dr. David Kevington was not there to receive it. He had moved on already, following what had seemed a strong but ultimately proved to be a false lead indicating that Brady Kenton and Victoria were in Denver.

The message, though, was picked up by one of two hired investigators who had been instructed to remain behind in St. Louis and keep a close eye on the offices and personnel of the *Illustrated American*, just in case Brady Kenton decided to come home.

They'd also been instructed to maintain a close vigil on the telegraph wires, in case any other promising information came through from other hired agents such as McCurden, who was following his own leads elsewhere.

The other agents knew that their British employer, virtually a stranger to them, put much stock in McCurden. The man had a record of success as a manhunter and was known to be willing to do whatever it took to achieve his purposes.

McCurden's wire from Culvertown was in the hand of one of the agents an hour after it arrived and forwarded on to Dr. David Kevington in Denver imme-diately afterward.

It was delivered to Kevington's hand as soon as it arrived.

Kevington, a tall, lean, intense man with a thick and unmoving mass of gray hair atop his head and eyes that could cut holes through anyone he chose to glare at, began his preparations for travel as soon as he'd read the wire.

The arrival of this wire at this time and place was a sign, surely, an indication that fate was on his side. Kevington had made a fruitless trip to Denver, fol-lowing a lead that had petered out to nothing. But now the journey had proven itself worthwhile after all. Be-ing already in Colorado, Kevington would be able to reach Culvertown much more quickly than if he were starting from St. Louis.

And the quicker the better. McCurden's wire said he had found Brady Kenton and Victoria, too.

CHAPTER

19

JACK LIVINGSTON POURED ANOTHER SHOT OF WHIS-key into the cracked mug that Brady Kenton had just drained. They'd been talking for an hour, and Kenton's voice was tired.

Livingston, never a man to sit silent for long, had done so while Kenton told his story. It was just too intriguing to interrupt.

Kenton had just finished describing his harrowing encounter with the now-dead son of David Kevington, who had come to the United States in pursuit of Rachel Frye because she was witness to a murder he had committed in England. Rachel Frye was the daughter of Brady Kenton, though he did not know of her existence until she tracked him down.

It was from her that Kenton had at last learned that his missing wife was still alive, living now as the spouse—and virtual prisoner—of David Kevington.

"Please . . . go on with your story," Livingston urged when he could stand the waiting no more.

Kenton swished the whiskey around in his mouth,

then swallowed and wiped his lips on the back of his hand. "The circumstances that I found myself in after Rachel and I were finally united allowed me to fake my death with relative ease, and with the cooperation of Alex Gunnison. With me officially dead, Rachel and I were free to travel anonymously to England. Rachel guided me to the Kevington estate, then went into hiding, at my insistence, at the home of some former Kevington servants who agreed to protect her and keep her presence secret . . . and to help her get away if I sent word for her to flee.

"I'll pass over the details and tell you simply that I did manage to get into David Kevington's estate. I found Victoria. . . . She was as overwhelmed at our reunion as I was. She hadn't known whether I was living or dead. She was eager to leave the prison of a home he had given her, and we tried to do it . . . but I was caught. Kevington locked me away, literally threw me in a cellar, and would have killed me right away had not Victoria begged him not to and told him she would take her own life if he killed me.

"A sympathetic servant in the household cooperated with me, and sneaked word from me out to Rachel that she should leave the country at once and come back to the United States. She did that, I was told . . . but now, God help me, I have no idea where she is or what happened to her. There was a boat accident off the coast, right about the time she would have been returning. . . . Dear God, I hope she wasn't on that boat." Kenton paused, poured himself another drink, and took two long sips before continuing.

"Though Victoria's protests might hold him back for a time, Kevington intended to kill me. I knew that. I was his prisoner, the man who had come to take away the woman he perceived as his wife, and even though he dared not do it directly because of Victoria, I knew it would happen. There would be an 'accident' of some sort, or a disappearance. I was doomed, unless I escaped. But I wouldn't leave Victoria.

"It was the same servant who delivered the message to Rachel who proved to be my salvation and Victoria's. At a great risk to himself, he arranged my escape and Victoria's. He even had a wagon and a driver to get us away.

"But it was a nightmare. Kevington pursued us, and with Victoria's condition, it was difficult to travel. Thank God that there are those in the world who will trust people based on their intuitions and give a hand to you even before they know all the answers.

"Through the help of good people and, surely, the hand of God himself, we made it to the coast and took passage to the United States. But we knew that Kevington would follow us. I've tried to deny it at times, but I can't. It was for that reason that I didn't even contact Alex Gunnison, my own partner, when we returned. I know that Kevington will try to get Victoria back, and if he can't succeed, then I believe he'll kill her, and me as well. He'll not be able to bear the thought of Victoria being alive but no longer his possession. And he'll not be able to bear the thought of me being alive at all."

Livingston tapped his fingers on the table. "We're

all in danger, then. Anybody who helps you, anybody who is close to you, anybody who can lead him to you."

"Yes. And I suppose it was wrong of me to put you in that situation, Jack. But I had to find a place to hide that would be remote and not easy to predict. Your place here was the closest I could come."

Livingston looked Kenton in the eye. "You know that Victoria's not fully yours yet."

It stung, but Kenton did not flinch. "Yes. I know."

"She stays in a room away from you. And I know she gets you all angry sometimes."

"Not angry. I could never be angry with her."

"Hell, if it ain't anger, it's something mighty like it. Why, you've sneaked down into town and got drunk two, three times since you've been here. And every time it's been after she shrugged you off."

Jack Livingston's forthrightness was not easy to take, not so much because it was brutally insensitive—which was typical of Livingston—but because it was brutally truthful.

"I know," Kenton said. "I shouldn't have done it."

"Hell, Brady, it was dangerous. You think that because your hair and beard are different people can't recognize you?"

"Look, Jack, I'm not going to defend myself on that one. You're right. I shouldn't have showed myself in town. But this is a hard time for both Victoria and me. There have been times she just can't bear my presence, and when that happens it hurts like a sword run through me. I've had to get out and away, or I couldn't stand it. Do you really think I can stay hidden away in here forever?"

"Brady, don't show yourself in town no more. I don't care how worked up you are. You don't know that you showing yourself in public hasn't already caused word about you to get out. For all we can know, Kevington has ears and eyes everywhere. A rich man can afford to buy all the ears and eyes he wants. And all the trigger fingers."

Kenton didn't mention the sketch on the envelope that he'd accidentally left in the Buckeye Cafe . . . and the fact that it had disappeared. That one worried him a lot. He could take pains to change his own appearance, but his work was as recognizable as ever.

Livingston was right. He'd been overly careless.

"I'll not leave again like that, Jack."

Livingston was thinking. "No. You will leave. We all will."

"What are you talking about?"

"There's another place we can go. Even more hidden than this one. It'll be a place we can hide Victoria a lot better and keep her safe until we know for sure how hard this damned British doctor will try or not try to get her back. My guess is he'll try hard."

"Where is this place?"

"Have you ever heard of a town called Caylee?"

"Yes, but the one I've heard of is abandoned. A ghost town."

"That's the town. It's over the Culver Mountain, about fifteen miles from here. Hard miles, just a mule trail, no good road. But there's a place there we can take Victoria. She'll be as hidden there as anyone can be."

"But a ghost town, Jack? I don't want Victoria to have to live in some run-down abandoned cabin."

"She won't have to." Jack Livingston leaned a little closer and lowered his voice, as if about to say something secretive in a crowded restaurant. "There's one house there that's not run-down at all. You can't tell it much from the outside, though."

"What the devil are you talking about?"

Livingston lowered his voice even more. "Uh, Brady, I might as well tell you, in case you don't know it already: I ain't exactly a saint. I've done some things that wouldn't win me a gold star at church of a Sunday morning."

"Well, all right."

"One of the things I've done is, I had something of an association with a certain woman who wasn't my wife . . . but she was the wife of another man. The mayor of Culvertown for some years, as a matter of fact, up until she died a couple of years ago and he moved off to Colorado Springs."

"What does this confession of yours have to do with a house in Caylee?"

"We would meet there. That's the point. Maude's husband was a fearsome jealous man. We knew we couldn't risk getting together here in Culvertown, not even here in my house. Too many prying eyes."

"Not to mention a wife of your own." Kenton's tone was icy. As a man who had missed his own wife for many years, he had little use for marital infidelity.

A married man should honor his wife, Kenton believed, and give himself to no other.

"My wife was dead before any of this happened,
Brady. I was never unfaithful to her."

"Glad to hear it."

"Anyway, Maude and me would meet over in Caylee. She'd claim to be off on a trip to see her sister,
who suffered terrible with the gout for many years,
but in fact she'd spend a good part of the time with
me in Caylee. There was a house there that I fixed up
good and pretty on the inside, though I left the outside
looking all weathered and run-down. You'd hardly
know unless you look hard that it wasn't just another
relic. The way it's situated, you can hardly notice the
place at all, anyway. But it's there."

"I'll be!"

"Maude's been gone for two years and I ain't had
cause to be at that house, but I did go by about six
months ago just to take a look at it. It's still in right
good shape on the inside. Victoria could be comfortable there, and hidden away where nobody is likely
to see her. There's nobody else at all living in Caylee."

Kenton pondered this. The idea was appealing.
Certainly not as a permanent arrangement, but as a
good one for the moment. In such a place Victoria
could grow strong again, and he could care for her
like he wanted to.

"What about food and so on?"

"I'd provide it," Livingston said. "I'd haul anything
you need in on a pack mule."

Kenton nodded slowly. "Jack, I think maybe that's an offer I'm inclined to accept. If Victoria is willing, that is."

"Then I'll help you. But the truth, Brady, is that I think the wisest thing you could do is go to the law. Just tell them your whole story and ask for protection."

"I've thought the same thing many a time. But there are uncertain things . . . and the fact that Victoria is scared to death to bring the law into the situation. Victoria is afraid that Kevington will somehow be able to use the law to his advantage. And mostly she's afraid . . . blast it, I may as well admit that *I'm* afraid, too . . . that if we show ourselves this early, Kevington will do something extreme. He'd rather have Victoria dead than taken away from him."

"You can't hide forever, Brady."

"I know. I know . . . and it worries me. Because I don't think Kevington will stop until he finds us . . . until either he has stolen Victoria back or both Victoria and I are dead."

At that moment there was a series of loud knocks on the front door.

CHAPTER

20

KENTON CAME TO HIS FEET, GLARING TOWARD THE door, then looking wildly at Jack Livingston.

Livingston got up more slowly, frowning. "It probably ain't nothing," he said. "People come up from time to time, wanting to meet me because I got this reputation of being a strange old hermit."

"Should you answer the door or let it go?"

Livingston gnawed at his lower lip, frowning some more as he thought about it. Another round of knocking rattled the door.

"Hell, I'm answering. I'd rather know it ain't Kevington than think it might be. If there's a problem on the other side of that door, then bring it on and let's deal with it." Livingston reached under his vest and brought out the small revolver he carried there. "I ain't answering it alone, though," he said, shaking the pistol.

Kenton produced a derringer from his own pocket. "I'm of the same mind as you, Jack."

Kenton and Livingston walked together toward the

front of the house, keeping their footsteps light so as not to forewarn whoever was outside of their approach. Kenton positioned himself so that he would be hidden when the door was opened.

"Who the hell is it?" Livingston bellowed through the door.

"My name is Billy Connery," came the reply, in an Irish brogue. "I work for the *Illustrated American,* and I think there may be someone here I need to see."

Kenton felt like going through the floor. The *Illustrated American* had tracked him down! Dear Lord, if they knew he was alive, knew he was here, what else did they know?

He wondered for a moment if this was a ruse. But he knew there was a Billy Connery working for the magazine, an Irish illustrator hired about the time of his own disappearance. Kenton had picked this up through simply reading the magazine itself. Connery worked with Alex Gunnison quite closely. And Alex was probably worried about Kenton because of his lack of communication with him. . . .

It all fell together in Kenton's mind. Alex Gunnison had launched a search for him, had somehow detected his presence in Culvertown, and had sent his new partner to find him. Maybe Gunnison himself was somewhere in town, too.

"Ask him to slide his identification card under the door," Kenton whispered. "The *Illustrated American* issues standard identification cards."

"I want to see some identification!" Livingston hollered through the door. "Prove to me you're with the *Illustrated American*!"

"Just a moment. . . ."

A couple of moments later, the edge of a card appeared under the door. Livingston knelt and picked the card up, glanced at it, and handed it to Kenton.

There were no images on *Illustrated American* credential cards, so Kenton could not match the name on the card, that of William Clive Connery, with the so-far unseen face on the other side of the door. But the card was the authentic item. The accent sounded real enough, too.

He handed the card back to Livingston. "Maybe we should let him in," he whispered. "I think this is all on the up-and-up."

"But how in hell did they track you here?" Livingston whispered back.

"I don't know. I think we're going to have to talk to him, though, and find out. If they could find us, so could Kevington."

Livingston nodded, then put his face close to the door. "Step back. . . . I'm opening this door. You come in slow and easy. I've got a pistol in my hand, and if I so much as don't like the way you look, I'll blow you straight to perdition! You understand me?"

"I do, sir. You have naught to fear from me."

Naught to fear from me. . . . Kenton frowned. It was as Irish-sounding a phrase as he had ever heard, spoken in a distinctly Irish manner.

Too Irish, maybe? Too distinct? Maybe that brogue

didn't sound quite authentic after all. He experienced a moment of doubt. . . .

But Livingston had opened the door by this point and was stepping back to let their visitor enter.

As he entered the house, McCurden tried to come across as nervous, harmless, and even a little scared.

Kenton, behind the door, had a chance to study the new arrival before the new arrival saw him. Something struck Kenton as not right. He'd never met Billy Connery and had heard no descriptions of him, but for some unexplainable reason this man didn't strike him as being authentic. Kenton wished that they hadn't opened the door, or at least that he had hidden himself more completely.

"Mr. Livingston, sir, I've heard much about you," McCurden said.

"Why are you here?"

"I'm looking for Mr. Brady Kenton, sir. I have reason to believe he may be here."

"Ain't you heard? Brady Kenton is dead."

"No, sir. With all due respect, we both know he's not. I was sent here to find him."

There was no point in playing games. Kenton would be seen at any moment anyway. He stepped out from the corner so suddenly that the newcomer drew in his breath sharply.

McCurden looked into the face of one of America's most famous journalists and couldn't suppress a smile and a hungry glitter in his eye.

"Hello, Mr. Kenton." He thrust out his hand. "Billy Connery. It's an honor to meet you."

Kenton did not want to shake hands with this man. Some inner alarm was sounding. But he shook the hand anyway.

"No one was to know I was alive," Kenton said, in no humor for preliminaries and false friendliness. "How did you know?"

"I was informed by Mr. Gunnison. I don't know how he knew."

"Gunnison the father or Gunnison the son?"

Everyone knew that Alex Gunnison was the partner of Brady Kenton, so he seemed the more likely choice. "It was Alex who told me."

"Alex told you . . . after I made him vow not to tell anyone?"

"He's concerned about you."

"How did he know I was here?"

The questions were growing harder. But it wouldn't matter much longer. This pair was about to experience a jolting encounter with the truth. "I don't know," McCurden said. "He didn't tell me."

Kenton stared hard at the newcomer. "Who else knows?"

"Dr. David Kevington knows. That's what has Alex worried. He's afraid Kevington might try to find you and take Victoria back. You do have Victoria, don't you?"

Kenton glanced at Livingston, whose look let him know that Livingston had the same suspicions he did.

"Tell me, Mr. Connery, how is Sarah?"

"Sarah?"

"Alex's wife."

"Oh, of course. Sarah is doing well."

"You've talked to her?"

"Not long ago, as a matter of fact."

"Did she mention to you that her name isn't Sarah, but Roxanne?"

McCurden glared at him. "And my name isn't Connery. It's McCurden."

He pulled a pistol from beneath his coat with unexpected speed and dexterity and aimed it at Livingston's face.

CHAPTER

21

FOR A MOMENT, EVERYTHING WAS FROZEN.

Then Kenton brought up his own derringer, ready to use it, but McCurden swung his pistol and knocked it from Kenton's hand. It clattered across the floor.

Kenton was astonished, also embarrassed. Being outmaneuvered by this younger and swifter man made him feel old and clumsy.

Livingston lunged at McCurden as he whipped the gun at Kenton, but again McCurden was too fast. He swung the pistol back and struck Livingston on the temple, very hard. Livingston let out a grunt and fell to his knees. McCurden brought up his foot and kicked Livingston in the forehead with his heel. The blow was tremendously powerful, knocking Livingston backward.

"No more!" Kenton said. "No more! You'll kill him!"

"Damn right," McCurden answered. And he kicked Livingston again, on the side of the head.

Kenton threw himself at him, but McCurden

dodged, then whipped him with the pistol. Kenton stumbled to the left, fell.

Victoria's voice came from upstairs. "Brady? What's happening?"

McCurden was kicking Livingston yet again. Then he reached under his vest and came out with a knife.

"No!" Kenton shouted. He scrambled to his feet.

McCurden tried to stab Livingston, but Kenton knocked him off balance just in time. The blade missed.

McCurden was limber and quick, however, and managed not to fall. He danced over Livingston's crumpled form and turned.

Kenton did not care at this point what happened to him. He had to stop McCurden at any cost, to keep him from getting to Victoria upstairs.

"Brady?" she called, her voice full of alarm. "Brady, what's happening?"

McCurden took two steps back, steadying himself. He raised the pistol and aimed it at Kenton.

"Freeze! Don't move an inch, you bastard! I'll kill you right here, then go up and kill her!"

Kenton could not find his voice. He stared at McCurden, eyes glaring with hate.

"But first, I kill him." And swiftly he raised the blade again, came down with his full body, and stabbed Livingston in the side. He left the blade where it stuck and was up again in a flash, laughing.

Livingston made a faint sound, moved a little, then was still. Kenton could tell from the sound of Livingston's last exhaled breath that he would not draw in another.

"I'll kill you," Kenton said, hardly able to comprehend what had just happened. "Whatever it takes, I'll kill you."

"No, you won't. You'll never have that opportunity. If anyone else dies here tonight, it will be you. Because I don't really need you, Kenton. It's the woman upstairs that I'm after."

"Kevington sent you."

"He did. But it's not Kevington I'm concerned about. I'm doing this for me."

"What are you talking about?"

"Kevington wants that woman back, Kenton. You don't know how bad he wants her back. He's hired agents, manhunters, a whole spiderweb of people looking everywhere you might be, following everyone you might try to contact . . . but it's me who found you. I'm the lucky one."

"I'll not let Kevington have her back. It won't happen."

"It's not up to you."

"How did you find me?"

"Never mind how I found you. The point is, I did. And as you can see"—he kicked Livingston's body—"there's nothing I won't do to get what I want."

"However much Kevington has paid you, I'll pay more."

"Kevington hasn't paid me yet. And believe me, even he has no idea how high the price is going to be."

Kenton understood. "You're double-crossing him. You're going to hold Victoria hostage!"

"You're a smart man, Kenton. Smart enough to figure that out, smart enough to have faked your own death, smart enough to have found your wife, smart enough to have stolen her away. But you've reached the end of wisdom. This is my game from now on."

Victoria appeared above, walking out of her room slowly, looking down over the balcony railing. She grew pale when she saw Livingston lying unmoving on the floor.

"Well, greetings, my lady!" McCurden called up. "It's indeed a pleasure!"

"Go back in your room, Victoria," Kenton said. "This is a dangerous man. . . . He's killed Jack."

McCurden laughed as Victoria withdrew quickly, the door closing behind her.

McCurden's smile went away. "You and me are going upstairs, Kenton. Your wife is going to tie you up, and then I'll tie her up, and then we'll wait for Dr. Kevington to arrive. He's already been wired."

"You'll not take her away from me. I've gone too far to get her, and waited too long."

"Too bad that none of that matters anymore, Kenton. Now move. Upstairs."

Kenton had to obey. He backed away, eye on the derringer on the floor, but McCurden chuckled and shook his head. "Forget it, Kenton. Keep in mind that I'm not required to keep you alive at all. All I need is Victoria. Though I'm thinking that Kevington might be willing to pay a nice bonus if he got you, alive, thrown into the bargain. I'm sure he'd enjoy disposing of you in his own way, slowly and painfully."

Kenton, fighting a fury that threatened to make him lose control, headed up the stairs. Everything seemed surreal. Only minutes before, Kenton had been seated, talking over plans with Livingston, feeling pleased at the prospect of a safer location for Victoria. Now Livingston was dead, he was hostage, and Victoria was cowering in her room, moments away from being a hostage herself.

Unless she wasn't cowering, but doing what Kenton hoped she was. . . .

They reached the door. Victoria had locked it, which annoyed McCurden. He kept his pistol leveled on Kenton while he stepped back and rammed the door hard with his heel, once, twice. The latch smashed apart, the door swinging open.

"Damn you, woman, I'll tie you all the tighter for that!"

These were his final words. Victoria was standing just inside the door, with the sawed-off shotgun that Livingston had given her for protection, just in case, in her hands.

She had never fired a shotgun before and squeezed down hard on the triggers, setting off both barrels at once. The recoil slammed her backward as the impact of the shot striking his chest sent McCurden flying in the other direction, out against the railing, over which he pitched and plunged to the floor, where he landed in a bloody heap.

Kenton rushed in and gathered up Victoria, who was stunned and bleeding slightly from the forehead. The shotgun had struck her there when it bucked up.

"Are you all right, Victoria? Dear God. . . ."

"Is he . . ."

"Oh, yes. Very much so."

She closed her eyes. He helped her scoot back against the wall, where she sat weakly, breathing hard.

Kenton went out to the railing and looked over at the two bodies below. He hoped against hope to see Livingston move, alive after all, but he did not.

But amazingly, McCurden did move, just a little. And his eyes opened, looking up at Kenton, an expression of disbelief on his face.

"I suppose you aren't quite as smart as you thought you were, Mr. McCurden," Kenton said.

McCurden's lips moved, but nothing passed them except blood. Kenton was looking into McCurden's eyes as they went cold and glazed and life departed.

Kenton went back to his wife and held her.

"What now?" she asked. "Will someone come?"

"I don't know. It depends on whether anyone heard the shotgun go off."

"Who was he?"

"He was hired by David Kevington. And Kevington is on his way here, he said."

"Oh, Brady, we have to leave!"

"We have to go to the law, Victoria."

"No, Brady. I'm too afraid."

"Things have changed now. There are dead men."

"No, Brady. Take me away from here. Don't take me to the law!"

"Victoria . . ."

"Please, I beg you! I've killed a man. . . . What if they don't believe what we tell them? I'm afraid of what the law will do. David always told me that if I left him, the law would be on his side . . . the law would bring me back to him."

"Victoria, I have no choice. We must go to the law. Men are dead here."

She began to cry. "They'll call me a murderer, Brady. They'll take me away from you."

"But if we run, Victoria, it will only make it all the worse."

"But nobody knows we're here, Brady. Nobody knows it but us."

"The man you shot to death tonight knew. And he said that Kevington is coming, so Kevington knows. . . ." Kenton quit talking. *Kevington is coming.*

Kenton would not argue further with her. The law would become involved, now that men had been killed. But perhaps it could happen later, not now. And perhaps he and Victoria could somehow escape detection. When Victoria's "resurrection" was finally known to the world, Kenton didn't want her name associated with a fatal shooting, even one as justified as this.

"What if David is already here, in town?"

"Surely he isn't." But Kenton could not be sure.

"The man was going to have us wait for him. David may be closer than we know. I want to go, Brady. I want to get away from here. But is there a place we can go?"

Kenton could not deny her plea. He would not go to the law. They would gather the meager possessions they had with them, take food from Livingston's pantry, stock up on weapons and ammunition, and wipe out any traces that would indicate Victoria's presence here. They would try to arrange the setting to make it appear that Livingston and McCurden had killed each other. A good investigator would be able to detect otherwise, but it was not likely that a little town like this one would have a good investigator.

"Yes, Victoria. There is a place we can go, if we can find it. A little empty town called Caylee, over the mountain. There is a good place to hide there; Jack told me about it just tonight."

They had to hurry; the sound of the shotgun blast would have been audible outside the house. Kenton hoped the isolation of the house had kept the shot from being heard all the way down in town, but he couldn't assume it had.

Kenton wrapped his arms around his wife, and she all but collapsed in his embrace. He was overwhelmed by a sense of protectiveness and a desire to do what she wished.

"When will we leave, Brady?"

"Tonight. Right now. I'll gather food and supplies and see what kind of horseflesh is in Jack's stable."

"Poor Jack!" she said, voice tightening. "Poor, poor Jack!"

"He was good to us, Victoria. He helped us when few others could have. And I'll be sorry for the rest of my days that us coming to him here brought him such misfortune."

CHAPTER

22

ALEX GUNNISON BENT HIS HEAD LOW AND LET THE brim of his hat deflect the worst of the gritty New York City rain. The day was gray and foggy, the rain penetrating and cold. Gunnison had always loved New York, thought it one of the most visually exciting cities in the nation, but today it was drab and ugly. And ominous.

He and Roxanne had just disembarked from a horse-drawn cab outside a white-painted Catholic-run hospital on a side street close enough to the bay to be bathed in the murky, organic scent of the ocean.

Battling the wind for possession of his hat, Gunnison managed to pay the cabbie, the tip generous enough to bring a smile and a tip of the cap.

"Come back around here in an hour," Gunnison instructed. "We may be waiting for you. If you don't see us, just drive on."

"Very good indeed, sir. I'll do that very thing." He clicked his tongue and gave a little shake of the reins.

The cab rolled on, and Gunnison took Victoria's

arm and raced through the rain and wind for the broad double doors, both of which were marked with the image of the cross. Under the recess that protected the doors, they shook off all the excess water they could.

Roxanne glanced around. "Alex . . . look. But be sly about it."

He followed her subtle gesture and glanced back across the street. A man sat under a shelter built to accommodate those waiting for cabs. He was reading a newspaper and seemingly minding his own business.

"A little wet to be sitting out and reading a newspaper, even under a shelter, don't you think?" she said.

"Maybe. You're thinking he's one of Kevington's agents?"

"He could be. Just like the man on the train."

This was a delicate moment. Despite Roxanne's impassioned claim that she had seen a man trying to peer into their private car during the journey to New York, she had been unable to identify him among any of the male passengers, and no sign of any further intrusions had taken place. Gunnison trusted his wife but was secretly wondering if she had simply misperceived something and set her imagination to running out of control.

"I suppose we can't know. We'll just have to be careful."

"I think we have to assume the worst," she said. "When we leave here, it shouldn't be by this door."

"How would Kevington know that Rachel Frye is

here?" Gunnison asked. "He would have no reason to post a man here unless he knew there was someone here who could attract Kenton."

"Maybe that man is the same one who was on the train. He may have followed us."

Despite his doubts, Gunnison could not rule this out. If Kevington was after Kenton it made sense that he would send men to watch those with whom Kenton had a history of association.

"Well, let's go in," Gunnison said. He reached up and knocked loudly on the door.

A few moments later it was opened by a stoutly built nun, who smiled at them welcomingly while also studying them closely and with no small amount of suspicion. In this part of the city, Gunnison supposed, it was essential to be careful about strangers who appeared on doorsteps. "How may I assist you?" she asked.

"My name is Alexander Gunnison. This is my wife, Roxanne. We've come to see one of your patients, a young woman named Rachel Frye."

"Yes, indeed. Miss Frye is still with us, and much improved now. She will be pleased you have come. She had asked that we contact you."

"Yes . . . I received the letter. She's better, you say?"

"Come and see her for yourself. She is ready to leave us . . . but she has had no place to go."

"She has a place now," Gunnison said.

"Good. I'm Sister Anna. Please come with me."

The hallway was tall and broad, thick with shadows, and cool. Yet it was an unexpectedly pleasant and secure-feeling place, particularly after the soggy coolness outside.

"What happened to her?" Gunnison asked.

"She was injured when the ship she was on sank off the coast. For a long time she was mostly senseless, sometimes awakening but never speaking, not at the beginning. But with time, care, and much praying, she began to improve. She told us who she was and asked that we contact you, Mr. Gunnison, and ask you to come here."

They turned a corner. "Here we are. Wait here in the hall a moment. . . . I'll go in and make sure she is ready to see you."

Gunnison took Roxanne's hand while they waited.

Sister Anna reemerged. "She will see you now."

Gunnison somehow managed to hide his shock when he saw Rachel. She was thin and pale, and if Rachel as she was now was much improved over what she had been when she came to this hospital, she must have been in bad condition indeed.

But she brightened when she saw Gunnison and extended her hand. He took it, squeezed it gently, and smiled at her.

"Rachel, I'm glad to see you, and I'm glad to hear that you're doing better. Please allow me to introduce my wife, Roxanne."

"I'm pleased to meet you, Rachel," Roxanne said, taking the lead. She extended her hand to the seated woman.

"You're very beautiful," Rachel said.

"And so are you," Roxanne replied, even though Rachel at the moment had only a shadow of beauty about her. "We're very sorry that you've been hurt."

"I'm much better now . . . but it was important for me to talk to you. I'm sorry you had to travel so far."

Gunnison turned to Sister Anna, who had followed them back into the room. "Might we talk to her in private?"

"Certainly. Call me if you need anything." She silently glided out of the room.

Gunnison turned to Rachel. "I know there is much to tell, much to talk about, but I want to ask one thing at the beginning: do you know where Kenton is?"

Rachel closed her eyes. "I had hoped you wouldn't ask that question, because it tells me that you don't know where he is, either."

"You've not heard from him?"

"No. Not since I was in England."

Gunnison pulled up a chair for Roxanne, then a footstool upon which he perched himself. "Tell us what happened, Rachel. From the beginning."

She spoke in a soft voice that grew steadily weaker because she was not used to talking for a long time.

She talked at first about the background of the voyage to England that she and Brady Kenton made—how through her Kenton had learned that his wife still lived as the "wife" and prisoner of Dr. David Kevington. Also because of her, Kenton very nearly died because of Kevington's son, Paul, but in the end Paul had been the one to die.

Kenton had taken advantage of his situation and allowed Alex Gunnison to present a story to the world of his "death" and, with the freedom that comes of no longer being believed alive, had gone to England with Rachel to find Victoria again.

Rachel briefly described their voyage, their landing in England, the journey to the estate of Dr. David Kevington.

Though Kenton was her father, she called him Kenton just like everyone else did, because that's the way Kenton liked it.

"Kenton did not allow me to even approach the estate," she said. "He said it would be unsafe and make it more difficult besides, because he would have to worry about getting both Victoria and me out. I stayed, in secret, in the home of a family nearby who had been servants for Dr. Kevington at the same time I was. Kenton disappeared into the estate . . . and seemed to vanish.

"I waited for days for him to reappear, or to send word, but none came. I was sure he was dead, but then a message was sent out of the estate. Kenton sent word that I should flee the country as quickly as possible, and come back to the United States, specifically to St. Louis. I was to contact you, then await his return with Victoria . . . if it was to happen at all.

"There was something about the message that scared me. It didn't seem to me that Kenton was at all sure he would return at all, and clearly he was in some sort of danger. He had been on the estate for days, which could only mean that he had been caught and detained there. But at least his message proved he was still alive. And I knew it was a valid message because I knew his script. It was written by his hand.

"I did what he told me, fled the area, found passage on a ship back to New York. Then there was a storm, and a shipwreck . . . and my next memory was being here. For a time I didn't even know where 'here' was. But my strength, and my memory, came back slowly, and as soon as I could, I had this hospital contact you. And now you've come."

"We've come. But we still know nothing of what happened to Kenton."

Rachel's eyes grew red and moist. "I had hoped you would come telling me that Kenton was home, with Victoria."

"I wish I had news. And perhaps soon I will. We have some indications that Kenton is in Colorado."

"Colorado? Why there?"

"We don't know. It's unexpected, and maybe that's the point. He may be hiding there."

Rachel sat up straighter and looked more vigorous all at once. "Hiding . . . from Kevington?"

"That would seem the likely candidate."

"That would indicate he may have brought Victoria home."

"Yes . . . and also that Kevington has pursued them. Maybe personally, or more likely through hired agents. Or perhaps both."

"He might be *here,* in this country?"

"I don't think he would let Victoria go without a fight, or a chase."

"But if Kenton is back in the country, why hasn't he contacted you? Why hasn't he come looking for me?"

"That's the question we've all asked. And I've got a friend in Colorado right now trying to find the answer."

"Have you heard from him?"

"Not yet . . . not that I know of, anyway. We've made arrangements for me to be telegraphed by him at a certain station here in New York. But so far we've not checked in at the station."

Roxanne spoke. "I think Kenton is not revealing where he is because he's afraid of endangering others around him."

"It seems to me he should feel safer making it all public," Gunnison replied. "Victoria would be safe."

"No," Rachel said with conviction. "If you knew Dr. Kevington, you would understand. He is not a rational man, not a safe man. I can understand why he would hide. And Victoria would know even better. As soon as Kevington knows where she is, she is in danger. And the public will not protect her. If David Kevington believes he has lost her, he will not care what happens to him. He would murder her before the eyes of the entire world and not care what the result was."

"Then Victoria and Kenton will only be safe . . ."

"When David Kevington is dead."

CHAPTER

23

RACHEL STOOD, SLOWLY AND LOOKING WEAK, BUT once upright she did not totter. She walked to the window and looked out into the rain.

"I want to leave here," she said. "They've been good to me here, but I'm tired of being in this room. And I have a feeling that there is danger. . . . I've had dreams in which David Kevington comes here, and appears right in this room. And even though I run, he's always there."

Roxanne rose and joined her at the window. "That will not happen, Rachel. Alex and I are taking you away from here. You'll go home with us."

Rachel smiled. Roxanne smiled back, then looked out the window and lost the smile.

"Alex, he's still there."

"Who?"

"The man with the newspaper. It's raining harder than before, but he's still there."

Gunnison went to the window and looked out. This time it wasn't so easy to dismiss his wife's concerns.

The man did look absurdly out of place, seated in an inadequate shelter in a pouring rain, staring at a newspaper that was growing more sodden by the moment.

"We'll take no chances," Gunnison said. "We'll leave here by a back way. And we'll find a different cab. The question is, though, if Rachel is really strong enough."

"I'm strong enough," she said. "I'll go now. Do you believe that man out there was sent by David Kevington?"

"Maybe so," Gunnison said. "We believe that he might have been on the train that brought us here and followed us from the station. But we'll shake him off. I'll try to get the cooperation of the good sisters as well, should he come inquiring."

Rachel withdrew and seemed to grow smaller and paler as she pondered the idea of being watched and pursued.

"How much do you have to pack?" Roxanne asked Rachel.

"What I have on and two dresses given to me by the hospital."

"The cost of your treatment will be paid by the *Illustrated American*," Gunnison said. "And we'll keep watch over you until we can reunite you with Kenton, and—we hope—Victoria."

The man in the shelter outside was named Morrisey, a name that had once garnered a lot of respect in the Davenport Agency for Detection Services, one of the leading detective agencies in the nation. A certain incident involving the disappearance of a key piece of evidence in a case—a small cache of jewels—had destroyed his career even as it enriched his pocketbook. A poorly played game of cards had made the enrichment short-lived, and from then on he had worked as an independent, contracting for whatever work he could find. It was unlikely that he'd ever again find the opportunity to get his hands on any money to compare to what he'd had so briefly, so he didn't try. The comfort he'd taken in wealth for that one short and glorious period he now found in whiskey.

As he sat on the soaked bench under the leaky shelter, holding a soaked newspaper in his hand, he was looking more forward by the moment to the minute he could leave his position and head for the nearest saloon. Part of him was ready simply to desert his job, which at present was most uncomfortable. But the money the Englishman was paying made this too lucrative a hire. He'd stick it out, no matter how wet he got.

Morrisey, though, had some serious doubts about this assignment. The Englishman just might be loco, with his talk of the legendary Brady Kenton really being alive even though the *Illustrated American* itself had reported his death. Supposedly there was a chance that Alex Gunnison and his wife, whom Morrisey was hired to track, might lead him to Kenton.

It seemed unlikely. Kenton's funeral had been a lavish and highly reported affair, visited by all kinds of dignitaries. Of course, there was the fact that Kenton had been cremated, so there was no body to be seen. And it was always possible that what had really been cremated was a good-sized dog or goat or something, with Kenton himself being alive and snickering while everyone wept over a bunch of animal ashes.

A more likely explanation was that the English doctor was simply crazy and his notion of a still-living Brady Kenton was a madman's figment. What else could it be, considering that Dr. David Kevington also seemed to believe that Brady Kenton's wife—who Kevington also apparently claimed as his own wife—was also still alive and with Kenton. It was absurd; everyone who knew anything about Brady Kenton knew that his wife had died in a train accident many years ago.

Madman or not, Kevington paid well. Morrisey would stick it out as long as he could and milk as big a fee as he could from the obsessive Englishman. And if by some miracle the good doctor's wild notions proved to be correct, maybe he could deliver up Kenton to him as well. Pondering the size of the bonus *that* would generate was enough to make Morrisey's mouth water.

Could it be that Brady Kenton himself was inside that hospital?

Morrisey vowed he wouldn't let this job slip out of his hands. He'd almost gotten himself caught aboard the train when Gunnison's wife saw him looking into their private car. From then on he'd been extremely cautious and somehow managed to evade being seen by them for the rest of the journey.

His newspaper was so soaked now that it looked

foolish to keep pretending to read it. Morrisey tossed it aside and simply sat on the bench, staring at the hospital and trying to look like nothing more than a common pedestrian who'd taken shelter from the rain.

Time dragged by, the rain slowing, then building again, then slowing, but never fully stopping. The cab that had carried the Gunnisons, and which Morrisey had followed, came rolling around again, slowing, but the Gunnisons never came out. Ten minutes later the cabbie made another go-around. Again no Gunnisons.

Morrisey began to grow concerned. But he made himself wait another hour. Still the Gunnisons did not emerge.

The rain stopped and the sun even managed to break through over toward the west. Morrisey could wait no longer. He rose and went to the door.

Sister Anna answered, smiling at him.

"Pardon me," Morrisey said, touching the brim of his hat and nodding a greeting. "I happened to be passing a couple of hours ago and thought I saw an old friend of mine, name of Gunnison, come in here with his wife. I had pressing business and couldn't stop to be sure, but now I'm finished and thought I'd drop in and see if they might be here. It would be good to see old Alex again. He's here visiting a friend or relative maybe?"

"Do come in, sir," Sister Anna said. "I'll go see if this gentleman you are looking for is here."

"All right . . . but if he is, don't tell him I'm out here looking for him. I'd like to surprise him myself, you see." In fact, Morrisey planned to slip out the door again if Gunnison proved to still be in the hospital. The last thing he wanted was to actually run into the man.

"Very well. Do have a seat on our waiting bench. I'll be back around to give you information."

He sat down, picking up a newspaper that chanced to lie beside him. If Gunnison or his wife should appear around the corner, he'd make sure to have his face hidden in the paper, just in case Mrs. Gunnison had caught a clearer glimpse of him on the train than he thought she had.

Ten minutes passed and Sister Anna did not return. It dragged on to twenty minutes, then thirty, and finally Morrisey rose and walked farther into the hospital, where he encountered another nun.

"Pardon me, Sister, but have you seen Sister Anna in the last few minutes?"

"No, sir, but I can find her, if you wish."

"Please do. She was to come give me some information about a man I saw entering the hospital, but it's been some time now and she's not done so."

"Please be seated again. I'll find her."

He didn't sit down but paced, restless and beginning to suspect something was up. Another ten minutes dragged by. He was about to plunge into the depths of the hospital and find Sister Anna on his own when she came around the corner.

She had no apologies for her tardiness. "I'm sorry, sir, but the man you are looking for isn't here," she reported.

"What? Where is he?"

"He and his wife departed, with one of our patients."

"Patients . . . male or female?"

"I'm sorry, sir, but we make it a practice to release no information regarding our patients except through a formal inquiry system."

"They couldn't have left. I'd have seen them coming out the door."

"You told me you were elsewhere on business. How could you see our door? But it doesn't matter; they left by one of our side entrances."

Morrisey swore bitterly, turned, and left the hospital on the run.

CHAPTER

24

THEY'D EVADED HIM. DELIBERATELY OR NOT HE couldn't say, but it didn't matter, because the point was they were gone and the trail was broken.

It would be hard to catch up to them again . . . but wait! That private passenger car of theirs . . . that's where they'd go.

He caught a cab and urged the driver to make the best time he could back to the same railroad station from which he'd departed earlier. The driver made a run fit for a racetrack, and Morrisey overpaid him by a good margin, not so much because he tended toward high gratuities as because he had no time to wait around for making change.

He ran to the rail yard and jumped a fence designed to keep the general public on one side.

There was the *Illustrated American* private car, separated from the train and shunted off onto a side holding track.

"You there, boy!" he shouted at a middle-aged

black fellow carrying a bundle of mail toward a train. "Come here a minute."

The man did so, laying down the bundle at his feet and looking glad to have reason to be rid of the Atlas-like burden for a moment. "What can I do for you, sir?"

"That car over there on the sidetrack was part of a train I rode in on."

"Was it? That's the private passenger car of the *Illustrated American* magazine."

"I know that. Just tell me if someone has come back to that car within the last hour or so! It's important."

"Oh, there ain't nobody on it, I can tell you. Ain't nobody allowed to be on the cars when they're side-tracked like that, except of course for folks working for the railroad. Truth is, sir, you ain't really supposed to be where you is right now, 'less you're a railroad man."

"You let me worry about that, boy. Tell me when that car will be reconnected and pull out again."

"I don't know, sir, but I'll go find out, if you'll watch my mailbag for me."

"I'll watch your damned mailbag! Now hurry! This is important!"

The black fellow nodded, scurried off, then slowed down as soon as he rounded the corner of the building and was out of sight. He plodded along deliberately, not about to hurry up for a man as rude as this one.

He saw a railroad detective and went to him. "There's a man who jumped the fence and took my mailbag from me, sir. He's still around the corner there, I think. I believe he's going to take that mail and go through it for money."

The railroad detective was gone in a shot. The black man pulled a cheap cigar from his pocket, lit it, and moved over to where he could hear the railroad detective giving the intruder some serious attention, threatening a trespassing arrest and maybe worse. The intruder was swearing and furious, denying vehemently any intent to steal the mail, and in the end managed to regain control of his temper and with an apology win the privilege of being allowed to leave without being taken into custody.

When he was gone, the black man finished his cigar, plodded back around the corner, and picked up the mailbag again. Hefting it onto his shoulder, he headed for the waiting car, humming a happy tune to himself.

"Boy," indeed! He was a workingman, and proud of it. It was the fence jumpers of the world, the kind who got themselves run off by railroad detectives, who were the "boys" of the world in his book.

So far this was turning out to be a nice day.

Morrisey was furious, and wishing he could get his hands on that black scoundrel and that railroad detective sometime when they weren't safe on the job! But he had bigger things to worry him now than a wounding of his pride. He had to find Gunnison's trail again or otherwise give up any hope of further gain from his madman employer.

He had the strongest notion that it was Brady Kenton whom the Gunnisons had gone into that hospital to fetch. Kenton himself . . . and if he could only get him and deliver him to Kevington . . .

That private railroad car remained his only potential point of reconnection with his quarry. He found a hidden place on the other side of the rail yard—beyond the fence and out of the domain of the railroad detective—and settled down to watch the car and hope that Gunnison and company showed up at it soon.

Miles away, in a passenger cubicle on a train that had pulled out of New York while Morrisey was still sitting in the leaky shelter outside the hospital, Roxanne Gunnison laid her cloak over a shivering Rachel Frye.

"Thank you, mum," Rachel said. "I don't know why I feel so cold."

"Because it's a wet day and you've gone from being a hospital patient in a chair to running through the rain to catch a train . . . and all the while hoping nobody is watching.

"Did we get away from him?" Roxanne asked Alex.

"I think we did. But we're going to give things one more twist just to make sure. We'll get off at the next station, visit the telegraph station to see if we've heard anything from Billy Connery, then catch another train. Maybe to Philadelphia. From there we'll catch a train to St. Louis. If anybody is following us, him or anyone else, we'll shake him off."

"I'm worried about Kenton," Rachel said.

"So am I," replied Gunnison.

They rode in silence to the next stop, then disembarked. As quickly as possible they entered the station and sat down in a corner, hiding themselves behind the moving crowd in the station. Roxanne sat close to Rachel, occasionally smiling at her reassuringly.

The telegraph station was in the next building. Gunnison walked over. Five minutes later, he was back.

Roxanne knew he had something just from the look on his face.

"There was a wire waiting for me. . . . Billy has found Kenton."

"In Culvertown?" Roxanne asked.

"Yes." He handed Roxanne the wire.

KB FOUND IN CULVERTOWN. LIVINGSTON HOUSE. PLEASE COME.

"Why 'KB'?" she asked.

"Just to make it a little more unlikely for anyone to think we're talking about Brady Kenton."

"What's the Livingston house?"

"A place Kenton wrote about, occupied by an eccentric fellow named Jack Livingston—a big mansion on a hill he built for his wife. Kenton did an excellent piece of work about him and the house. And I think he may have hinted once that there was some sort of family connection between Livingston and himself, or Livingston and Victoria. I can't remember which . . .

and my memory may be entirely wrong on that score, anyway. It's murky for me."

"If there is a family relationship, it might explain why Kenton chose Culvertown as his hiding place," Roxanne said.

"I've got to get there, as soon as I can," said Gunnison.

"What about me and Rachel?"

Gunnison shook his head. "I don't know. I'd thought of taking you home to St. Louis, but now I'm not sure. If Kevington is having us watched, followed . . . you know he'll have spies observing our house and the *Illustrated American* offices. I don't want to leave you there if I'm gone."

"Take us with you."

"I don't know that Rachel is strong enough."

Rachel said, "I am strong enough . . . and if Kenton is there, I want to join him."

Roxanne looked at the telegram again. "We can't tell from this whether he has Victoria with him."

"My fear is that he doesn't," Gunnison said. "My fear is that he found she was dead, or unwilling to join him, and he came back to the United States alone, and maybe intent on drinking himself to death. I wish Billy had given more information in that telegram."

"Will you take us to Colorado with you?" Roxanne asked.

Gunnison grinned. "I guess there would be no easier way to keep an eye on you . . . and you on me . . . than having you with me."

"I'm glad. That's the way it should be."

"What we find may not be pleasing. Kenton may be in bad shape. Victoria may not be there at all, and may even be dead."

"How delicate do you think I am, Alex? This is something we should do together. And though I've had my share of resentments toward Kenton because of all the times he took you away from me, I want to be there to help him if he needs it. I care about him, too."

CHAPTER

25

ROY RAMSEY, UNDERPAID AND OVERBURDENED TOWN marshal of Culvertown, Colorado, fell back into his chair heavily, making it creak. He threw his hands upward and shook his head.

"Tell me, Jim," he said to James Ramsey, his brother, who held no official capacity but helped fill in for Roy when he was out of town. "How is it that I can go to Scallonville for two days and come back and find the whole town gone to hell?"

"It's amazing, Roy. I'll grant you that."

"Tell me if I've got this straight: there were two dead up in the Livingston house, including Livingston himself."

"That's right."

"Shot to death."

"Yes. It looks to me like they shot each other."

"Who was the other one?"

"Stranger in town. I don't know that we'll ever find out."

"Where are they now?"

"In the undertaker parlor, stinking to high heaven. We got to get them buried fast."

"I'll take a look at them. But I'll probably not be able to figure out anything more than you did."

"We need some big-city police folks looking at this one."

"Well, we ain't got none of them. I'll look at them and we'll bury them. Hell, I never liked old Livingston much anyway."

"Why would anybody shoot him, though?"

"A dozen reasons. Attempted robbery, probably. You know the stories about him stashing money everywhere."

"There was some sign that a woman had been there. I found a hairpin and a woman's brush up in one of the bedrooms."

"Not surprising. It wouldn't be the first time old Jack had a woman. You know he had a big love affair going with the mayor's wife for a long time. But he would see her over in Caylee in an old house he fixed up. He thought nobody else knew about it, but everybody did. Including the mayor, but he didn't care. He had a woman of his own visiting him while his wife was visiting Jack."

"Maybe the woman he had up there lately had a husband who wasn't so go-along about all that kind of thing."

"Maybe."

"Are you going to investigate it?"

"Hell, no. I can't bring 'em back to life, can I? I figure they must have had a reason for shooting each other. That's good enough for me. Besides, if I solve the murder, what good is it? There's nobody left alive for the district attorney to prosecute."

"What about the first two dead men?"

"No witnesses. Two highway robbers . . . nothing there worth looking into, either. Whoever killed them did the world a favor." He shook his head and gave a wry laugh. "Damn, I can't believe this. Two dead men on the road as I leave town, and two more dead men when I come back."

"That ain't all. There could be a third one."

"What? Who?"

"Another stranger. A young man. He was found stabbed in an alley, nearly dead. He should rightly have been dead six times over, given the shape he's in, but he's still alive, or was the last time I checked. Not conscious, though. He's up at Doc Asheman's. The doc swears he's going to make sure this one comes through alive. Sort of a personal mission."

"No clue who stabbed him?"

"Not a one."

"Anybody identified this stranger?"

"Tell you the truth, I ain't tried. What am I going to do? Line up everybody in town and have them file by?"

"Reckon not. Well, if he lives, he can tell us who did it. If not, he's just corpse number five in a week unusually rich with them."

Billy Connery opened his eyes and stared at the ceiling.

Still alive, he thought. *I can't believe it. Still alive.*

Alive, but so weak he could not move, and his throat slashed so that he could not speak.

Billy Connery had no memory of the stabbing beyond its initial moments. The throat cutting in particular was absent from his mind, for which he was thankful. He figured he had been unconscious when it happened.

He said a prayer of gratitude every time a drawn-in breath made his throat burn. It had always been his belief that a slashed throat meant death. Apparently McCurden just hadn't cut quite deep enough.

But his stab wounds had done enough damage to leave Connery incapable of doing anything but lying here, worrying about what McCurden had done.

He'd talked about Kenton, and that was frightening. As best Connery could figure it, McCurden was probably an agent for Kevington.

Connery suffered in a frustration he was too weak even to show on his face. He had to get his strength back, had to get up to the Livingston mansion.

If only he'd done it when he had the chance.

As the sun edged toward the mountaintops to the west, Dr. David Kevington stood in a window on the second floor of the Culvertown Hotel and looked out across a scene of squalor that reconfirmed to him every hatred and prejudice he possessed regarding Americans. In Kevington's view, Victoria was the only worthwhile colonial product. And nothing less

than Victoria could have made him visit this miserable nation again.

He scanned the dirty street below, the buildings
that seemed even dirtier with their peeling paint and
layers of hoof-splashed mud extending more than a
yard up their fronts. And most were false fronts,
which Kevington found irksome and typically American. The entire American culture was in his mind
something of a false front, something pretending to
be much bigger and grander than it was.

Damn them all. He wished he could fetch back his
Victoria, head back to England, and leave the entire
North American continent in flames. He'd never fulfill
that fantasy . . . but one he would fulfill. He'd not
leave this rubbish heap of a country until Brady Kenton was dead.

And if Victoria refused to come with him willingly,
then he would leave her dead as well. Painful as it
would be, he would do it. He would not be mocked.
He would not be denied.

Kevington lifted his eyes and gazed at the looming
Livingston mansion. From his pocket he pulled the
copy of the telegram McCurden had sent:

K. AND V. FOUND CULVERTOWN, COLORADO. EN-
TER CULVERTOWN HOTEL AND AWAIT WORD.

Well, here he was, but so far there was no visit
from McCurden, no word from McCurden. Curse him
for the fool he was! His message had been inadequate.
He should have given some indication of how to con-

tact him. But if in the end McCurden delivered what his telegram promised, Kevington was prepared to be quite forgiving.

He saw Bartholomew Graham striding across the street toward the hotel. Graham was an interesting man to observe: tall and wide and muscled and bearded, he looked somewhat like a cleaned-up but still unshorn mountain man. Graham's looks were almost stereotypical of the American frontier, and Kevington had found it amusing to watch the reactions of Americans the first time they heard Graham speak in a voice rich with the dialect of his native Essex. Graham might look like an American frontiersman, but he was British to the core and proud of it.

He was also heartless, smart, and willing to do whatever Kevington paid him to do, and those were key reasons Kevington had brought him along from England to help with the great chase. An additional reason was Graham's four years of roaming in the American West, hiring out his gun to whoever paid the highest and had the fewest scruples.

Kevington was awaiting at the door of the room when Graham came lumbering up the stairs.

"Anything?" Kevington asked.

"Not one bloody clue," Graham replied. "Nothing solid, anyway."

"Damn!" Kevington exclaimed, stepping aside as Graham entered the room and threw himself down on a chair. Kevington closed the door. "Where the devil could McCurden be?"

"He may be dead."

"Why do you say that?"

"There's apparently been an epidemic of violent death in this town of late. So go the stories in the pubs, in any case. Two highwaymen shot dead on the road into town and two other dead men in the big mansion up on the hill."

"Who were these men?"

"The two highwaymen were a pair known to plague the region, haunting the roads to several towns and camps. One of the dead men in the mansion was the man who owned the dwelling . . . quite an eccentric, it seems. The other, though, was a stranger to folks here. It could be our own McCurden."

"Or anyone else. It had better not be McCurden. If he's gone, then it will be hard indeed to learn what he found."

"The dead man could have been Kenton, too."

"He could have been Paul the Apostle for all we know. More than likely he was just a burglar who was confronted by the owner of the house, and both of them wound up dead."

"I'm sorry I've got nothing more to tell you," Graham said, pulling a pipe and pouch from his pocket and beginning to prepare a smoke. "Perhaps the others will do better."

"Perhaps they will," said Kevington, looking out the window again. "They're coming this way now . . . and they've got a boy with them."

CHAPTER

26

WHERE GRAHAM HAD A CERTAIN ENGLISH GRACE about his manner, despite his burly build, George Evaline and Kendall Brown were Americans, products of poverty and violent households, and as rough-edged as men could be. Both were lean, flinty-eyed, and even more unscrupulous than Graham but were loyal to those who paid them. Upon his arrival in the United States, Kevington had hired an underground agent to assemble him a little army of investigators and hired toughs, and Evaline and Brown had come with the highest recommendations.

"Who's this?" Kevington challenged Brown as he threw open the door, gesturing toward the boy with them. The boy wore a smart, disdainful expression and had the butt of a reeking cigar smoldering on his lip. He strode into the room like he owned it, Kevington glaring at him and instantly disliking him.

"That's Stockton Shelley," Brown said. "Local boy . . . he says he knows some things about Brady Kenton."

"What I know I'm glad to tell," Stockton said. "For the right price."

Kevington knelt and looked into the boy's face. Smiling, he reached up and removed the cigar from his lips and handed it to Evaline, who took it to the window and tossed it out.

"Cheap tobacco is rather revolting," Kevington said. "So are little boys with exalted views of themselves."

"You're foreign!" Stockton said, not at all cowed by Kevington's menacing manner. "Where the hell you from? France?"

"England, young man. The mother country of this vast wasteland of yours. Now, tell me what you know about Brady Kenton."

"I know he drawed some might pretty pictures in his day. Anything else I know about him don't come free."

Evaline stepped forward, ready to grab the boy and begin persuading him to change his mind. But Kevington shook his head and waved him back.

"I'm not inclined to pay for that which may prove worthless," Kevington said to Stockton.

"Then I reckon you'll never know," Stockton said, pulling another cigar from his pocket and sticking it in his mouth. It was a cheap saloon cigar, the kind barkeeps sold for a nickel out of jars. Stockton turned to Graham, who was puffing on his pipe. "Got a match, *compadre*?"

Graham laughed as he pulled a match block from

his pocket. He liked this boy. "Here you are, young man."

"Well, well! Another Frenchman!" He fired up the cigar and blew the smoke toward Kevington.

Graham laughed heartily. "You know, young gentleman, I've killed men for lesser insults than that one."

"I don't believe you'll want to kill me. Not if you want to know where to find Brady Kenton."

"You have this information, I take it?"

"Wouldn't be talking about it if I didn't."

"You have a wiseacre attitude about you, young fellow. Do you have any notion how serious a matter we are talking about here?"

With a gesture toward Evaline and Brown, Stockton said, "I know that these two were going around asking whether anybody knew where Brady Kenton was. Most folks laughed and told them to look in the graveyard. But me, I know better. I can tell you where he's been . . . and where he is now."

"A big claim."

"Needs some big money to go with it."

Kevington had never met a boy he disliked more, and he disliked all children. But right now he was short on leads. McCurden had not appeared. Urchins of the street sometimes did know things worth knowing. He'd put up with the boy for now, in case he really did know something.

"If you can lead me to Kenton, my boy, it's worth a hundred dollars to me."

Stockton Shelley's bravado couldn't hold up. His

eyes widened and it was clear at once that he hadn't expected an amount like that. To Stockton, a hundred dollars was a rich man's fortune.

"I'll lead you to him," he said. "And I hope you get somebody to arrest him, because he's a murderer."

"What do you mean?"

"He killed two men up in the Livingston mansion."

"How do you know it was Kenton?"

"Who else could it be? He was up there in that house."

"How do you know?"

"I seen him."

"Was there a woman, too?"

"You're the second man to ask me that. I never saw no woman. But if she was in the house, I wouldn't have seen her."

"Who is in the house now?" Kevington asked.

"Nobody that I know of."

"Who was the second dead man?"

"I don't know. But I know it wasn't Kenton."

"How do you know that?"

"Because I seen Kenton, traveling."

"Alone."

"No. Not alone. There was a woman."

"You told me you never saw a woman with him!"

"I told you I never saw a woman with him the *first* time I saw him." Stockton smirked.

"Damn you, boy, I'll not have you play games with me! I don't know that I believe a word you're telling me."

Graham spoke. "If that big house on the hill is

empty, I think we should go in it. If Kenton and Victoria have been there, maybe there will be some sign of it."

"You said you saw Kenton traveling, boy. Where was he going?"

"All I can say is what he seemed to be going toward."

Kevington reached into a pocket. His hand closed around a derringer that he was ready to pull out and shove into the boy's face. But instead he took a deep breath, put his face closer to Stockton's, and said in an icy tone: "Listen to me, young man. I don't know you, and I don't know whether you are telling me the truth. But I have the strongest sense that you think you are very clever indeed, and that all of this is quite the game. Let me tell you something, my boy. I am not a gentle man. I am not a friendly man. I am not a man who has an abundance of scruples. If I find that you are indeed toying with me, I will personally cut off your ears, one at a time, and send you home to give them to your father and mother for whatever use they may want to make of them. Have I made myself clear?"

Stockton lost his smirk. "Yes, sir."

"Now . . . we will go to this house, and look it over. If we find evidence that Kenton and Victoria have been there, your credibility will rise. But you will tell me—now—where it is you believe Kenton has taken her."

"I'm thinking, sir, that maybe he's taking her to the ghost town across the mountain, a town called Caylee.

There's a house there that Livingston kept up for staying in. I think Kenton killed Livingston and headed for that other house."

"And why would Kenton kill Livingston and some stranger?"

"I don't know. Maybe he was trying to protect the woman or something."

Kenton as a killer. Kevington thought it over and found it perfectly plausible. God knows he himself would gladly kill for Victoria. Kenton would probably do no less.

"Let's go," Kevington said. "I want to look through that mansion. Is it locked up?"

"I know a way in," Stockton said. He was being cooperative now, not nearly so snide and cavalier. Kevington had scared him, almost enough to make him run.

The only thing holding him back was that he didn't have his hundred dollars yet.

CHAPTER

27

THE LIVINGSTON MANSION WAS ALWAYS A DARK AND ominous place but now was all the more uninviting because two men had died bloody deaths there.

Kevington stood looking up at it, with Stockton at his side. The boy's usual cocky attitude was gone now, driven away by a fear of Kevington and his toughs that he tried unsuccessfully not to show.

"How are we going to get inside?" Evaline asked.

"Break out a window," Graham said.

"You don't have to do that," Stockton replied. "I know some secret ways into the house. It was built with secret ways in and out because old Livingston's dead wife liked that kind of thing."

He led them around the rear of the mansion and into a root cellar that was built right into the hillside and nearly hidden in a tangle of foliage and scrubby trees that had been allowed to have their way unmolested for years.

"It's in there."

"What is?"

"The door to the tunnel."

Indeed there was a door hidden inside, on the rear wall. It was designed to blend into the structure in a natural way and had no apparent latch. But Stockton pushed one board, which tilted out and revealed a latch beneath. He tripped it easily.

"Did the man who owned this place know you made yourself such free and easy entrance to his dwelling?" Kevington asked.

"Old Livingston never used this tunnel, and I never went all the way into the house except once, when I knew he was gone. I'd come up here and hide in the end of the tunnel, mostly."

"Hide from what?"

"My father. When he gets drunk, he beats me."

Kevington grunted. He was not a sympathetic man. "Well, I'll be the one to beat you if all this proves unworthy of the effort."

"You wanted in the mansion, I'm getting you in the mansion."

By match light they proceeded into the dank and earthen tunnel, bending low in the claustrophobia-inspiring place. Soon, though, they reached a door similar to the one that had admitted them. Stockton triggered the latch.

They entered a cellar so dark it was distinguishable from the tunnel itself only by the sense of open space around them. Graham struck another match, and by its light they saw and proceeded toward the flight of stairs leading to the main floor.

Stockton still led the way, being familiar with this house.

"There's all kinds of other passages and tunnels and such," he said, much like a tour guide. "Old lady Livingston was crazier than her husband and liked stories about tunnels and towers and passageways and all. That's what everybody says, anyway."

"Honestly, young man, I couldn't give a tinker's damn about the history of this house or the relative sanity of those who built and occupied it," Kevington said. "I want to know only two things: whether Brady Kenton was here alone, or with my Victoria, and where the pair of them are now."

The stairs led them into a rear hallway. Stockton led them to the main room. "There's some lamps and candles around if you want light."

"Candles will suffice," Kevington said. "I don't want much light to draw attention from the outside."

They lit three candles among them and moved through the room, examining the bloody places on the floor where the bodies had lain. Though Stockton found it fascinating, the men weren't much stirred by the sight. They'd drawn enough blood themselves over the years to take little interest in it now.

"Where are the bedrooms?" Kevington asked.

"Upstairs," Stockton replied.

They climbed and began to explore the rooms. It was evident which one had been Livingston's. It was packed and dirty and disordered, the room of a man who had lived for a long time without the organizing influence of a female. They found the room Kenton had been in as well but did not realize it because he had left no identifying traces behind.

In the largest of the bedrooms, however, they found two items of significance: a woman's brush and a ruby-tipped hairpin that Kevington recognized as Victoria's. He held it in his hand and for the first time exhibited visible excitement.

"She was here," he said firmly, then repeated it twice, each time with more emphasis on the final word. "That bastard Kenton took her all the way from England, took her from me, and thought he could hide her here in this damned little mountain mining town . . . but he failed to take into account the determination of his adversary. I've tracked them down! He thought he could hide from me, but I've tracked him down like a hound on the trail of a fox! Ha!"

"Seems to me that some of us had a bit to do with tracking him down, too," muttered Evaline, with a glance at Kendall Brown.

Kevington paced about the room, brows knit and mind racing. "I think I know what has happened here. Kenton is so desperate to hide his trail that he's taken to killing. He's murdered his own host and taken away Victoria to an even more remote hiding place. He's so determined to keep Victoria for himself that he's killing anyone who knows he has her. But I'll track him down. And when I do, it will be Kenton who dies."

"Begging your pardon, Doctor, but Kenton may already be dead," said Graham. "Remember that there were two men killed in this house. I figure the second one was Kenton. Almost nobody knows that Kenton didn't really die last year, so nobody would recognize the dead man as Kenton even if it was Kenton. They'd just assume it was somebody who happened to resemble him. All we've got is this boy's word that he's seen Kenton alive since then. And I figure this boy is saying whatever he thinks will make him a dollar. I've been thinking, and I've got a theory. I believe McCurden tracked down Kenton and your woman, murdered Kenton and the man who owned this place, and took Victoria away somewhere else to hold her for ransom. I expect you'll hear from him before long, making a big demand."

Kevington thought about this, eyes glaring in anger. "If he's done such a thing, I'll see him suffer a good long while before he dies."

Evaline spoke. "Seems to me what we've got to find out is who this second dead man is. If it's Kenton, then we can assume that McCurden's probably got the woman with him somewhere. If it's McCurden, then we can figure the kid here is probably telling us the truth, and Kenton's gone with his woman to the ghost town."

Kevington wheeled and faced him. "Don't ever refer to Victoria as Kenton's woman. Don't ever say that again. Do you understand me?"

"Mighty sorry, sir. I misspoke."

Kevington nodded. "Yes . . . but you have a point. We need to learn who died here besides this Livingston gent."

"They got a morgue in this town, boy?" Brown asked Stockton.

"Just the undertaking parlor."

"Maybe the corpses are still there," Kevington said.

Graham stepped forward. "I'll go see. I've seen Kenton's picture enough to know his face, and I met McCurden when you hired him. I'll go and settle this matter for us . . . if the bodies are still in the morgue."

"A good idea, Graham," Kevington said. "We'll await you."

"At the hotel?"

"Right here."

"What about the boy?" Evaline asked.

"He stays with us, until we're through with him."

This was fine with Stockton, who spent many nights away from home when his father was drinking. It usually took three or four nights away from home before his father came looking for him. If he was lucky, he wouldn't come looking tonight. Stockton right now had one goal: to do whatever it took to see this through to the end and get his hundred dollars.

"I'll be back," Graham said, readying to go.

"Don't rouse too many questions," Kevington said. "Attention is not what we want."

"I'll be careful," Graham replied.

CHAPTER

28

GRAHAM WALKED SLOWLY THROUGH THE DARKEN-
ing town, smiling and tipping his hat at the women
he saw and nodding politely to the men. Rough and
rugged as he looked, he was in fact quite smooth in
his manners, even charming when he wanted to be.

His charm vanished, though, when he rounded a
corner and was run into by a staggering drunk who
carried a glass of beer in his hand, taken from a
nearby saloon when the barkeep wasn't looking. The
beer splashed down Graham's front—and the drunk
roundly cursed him, as if it were all Graham's fault.

Graham smiled, but it was a smile to put fear into
the heart of the man on the receiving end of it. The
drunk found himself grabbed by the collar, his face
dragged close to that of Graham.

"My good friend," Graham growled in his English
accent, "I suggest you voice your apologies for your
bad behavior right away, or I'll draw out my knife,
gather a crowd to watch the show, and castrate you

right out there on the street. And my knife is a very dull knife, I might add."

The drunk stared into the Englishman's fierce eyes, slobbered down his chin, and nodded. "All right, mister. All right. I'm mighty sorry."

"Are you now? Sorry, might I ask, for spilling your beer all down me or sorry for making such an ass of yourself immediately thereafter?"

"Uh . . . both."

"Not good enough, sir."

"What?"

"I want you to *show* me you're sorry. See that puddle of beer at my feet?"

The eyes shifted down, then back up. "Yeah."

"Lap it up. Like a dog."

"There's . . . there's folks watching."

"Indeed there are." Graham shoved him away, then drew his pistol. "Would you prefer those folks see you cleaning up your spilled beer or bleeding out your last moments with a bullet in your belly?"

The drunk, trembling, slowly got on his knees. He glanced around, humiliated, then lowered his head and began to lick lightly at the puddle of beer on the boardwalk.

"Oh, come now!" Graham said. "You can do better than that! Lick that boardwalk like you mean business!"

"Folks spit down here," the drunk murmured.

Graham put his foot on the back of the man's neck and shoved his face down so hard onto the walk that it almost broke his nose. "Drink, you cur!"

The drunk licked the boardwalk with full swipes of his tongue while men gathered around and laughed.

Graham was satisfied. "Keep at it until it's all cleaned up," he instructed his victim. Then he turned to the nearest watcher and said, "Might you point out to me where the mortician's establishment is?"

The drunk pulled up and back clumsily, almost rolling over. "Don't kill me!" he begged.

Graham looked at him with disgust. "Get on with you, you miserable sod. I've had all I can stand of looking at you!"

The drunk somehow made it to his feet and headed off down the boardwalk, then cut left into the dark safety of the nearest alley. Catcalls and laughter followed him.

Graham received directions to the undertaking parlor, but the man added, "The place is probably closed right now. But the undertaker lives in rooms up above it."

"Then I'll roust him out if need be. Thank you, sir, for your aid."

Graham walked on, whistling, receiving wide berth from those he passed.

Now that he was alone, the drunk in the alley got his courage back. "Reckon you'll not do that to me again!" he muttered beneath his breath. "Reckon next time I'll know how to deal with you, you damned foreigner!"

But he knew that it would be for the best if there

wasn't a next time. The Englishman had a dangerous manner about him.

As he calmed down, the drunk's anger began to change to maudlin sorrow. He'd been humiliated before the people of his own town! Forced to lap up spilled beer off a filthy boardwalk! He even had a couple of splinters in his tongue.

There was surely no one in the world more miserable than he, no one more despised by man and God. He began to sniff and whimper and wish he had more beer . . . in a glass rather than spilled, preferably.

He began to think back on the times his family had been together and his home was happy. Now his wife was gone, his life was miserable, and most of the time he didn't even know where his son, Stockton, was or what he was doing. The boy would wind up a convict one day with his roaming, stealing ways! Just another reason to feel sorrowful and self-pitying.

He decided to find Stockton. Bring him home. Maybe they could sit and talk or play a game of cards or do something like fathers and sons are supposed to do together. He hoped Stockton never found out that his father had been forced to drink beer off the boardwalk.

Josiah Shelley exited the alley by its rear entrance and vowed that he would not go home again until he'd found Stockton. He and the boy would have a good time together . . . and if Stockton had something cocky to say about it, he'd quick learn the better of it! Sometimes the only way to do good for that boy was to beat it into him.

Josiah wandered through the dark streets, trying to think of the various places Stockton liked to hide.

Graham returned to the mansion an hour later.

"Well? Did you see the bodies?" Kevington asked.

"Both already buried," Graham replied.

Kevington swore.

"But I know who the second dead man is, anyway. I persuaded the undertaker to show me his personal effects . . . including this. Recognize it? I managed to sneak it away unnoticed."

He held out a brass matchbox with initials engraved on its top. Kevington took it and studied it.

"McCurden's. So our agent in Culvertown is dead," he said. "Killed, no doubt, by Brady Kenton, who then fled with Victoria."

"So it would seem."

"Tomorrow morning we travel to this ghost town across the mountain. And before the sun goes down tomorrow, I will have Victoria with me again, and Brady Kenton in his grave."

"What about tonight? Do we return to the hotel?"

"The accommodations here are much more comfortable. We spend the night right here in this house . . . where Victoria has been."

"I left some things at the hotel," Brown said.

"Then go back and get them . . . cautiously. Don't let anyone see you leaving or reentering this house. Bring back everything any of us have left at the hotel, then try to get some rest. I want us all to be at our best tomorrow. Kenton will resist. He'll not surrender Victoria lightly."

"He can resist all he wants. It won't do him any good in the end," Graham said.

"No," Kevington agreed. "It won't. I'll not leave this country without her. Either Victoria is mine . . . or she is no one's."

"And what if she doesn't want to go back with you?" It was a question only Graham was bold enough to ask.

Kevington glared at him. "She will see what she should do when the time comes. She'll come back."

"And if she didn't . . . you'd kill her?"

Kevington had nothing further to say.

CHAPTER

29

Josiah Shelley was growing tired. And for the first time in a long time, he was worried about Stockton. Usually Josiah never bothered to think about him, much less worry about him . . . but never before had he been quite so hard to find.

Over time Josiah had learned most of the places Stockton frequented when he was away from home—at least half the time anymore. Tonight he'd checked all of those places, and no Stockton. Where could the boy be?

He paused, looking up at the Livingston mansion, and realized there was one place he hadn't yet looked. Stockton had been known to hole up sometimes in one or the other of the tunnel entrances to the mansion. Maybe he was there.

If so, Josiah was almost inclined to leave him. He'd always thought the mansion was a dismal and haunted-looking place; he seldom looked at it by night without feeling a chill on the back of his neck. Now that the place had been sullied by two shooting deaths, it seemed even more frightening.

But he screwed up his courage and strode off toward the house anyway. His resolve to find his missing son was high tonight, heightened because of the humiliation he'd experienced earlier. Tonight he needed to do something he could be proud of, even if only finding his straying boy.

He circled around the back of the mansion, heading for the root cellar that was actually the entrance to the tunnel Stockton seemed to favor most as a hiding place.

Stockton Shelley was asleep, curled up on a sofa in the big parlor of the Livingston mansion, and dreaming that his father was calling him.

He cowered deep into the soft sofa. When his father called, it usually meant a beating was soon to come. Stockton murmured in his sleep and actually, through some subconscious awareness that he was dreaming, tried without success to wake up.

"Stockton! Are you here?"

His father's voice was closer now, louder, more vividly imagined than before. Stockton's heart raced.

"Stockton! Boy, are you hiding in this house? I believe you're here! Did you think I wouldn't find you? I know about the tunnels as well as you do, boy! Don't forget it!"

Stockton opened his eyes, then sat up.

Something large and dark passed him, a shadow sweeping past the sofa.

"Stockton, is that you?"

Stockton could not speak. He was terrified, and not of his father. The shadow he'd seen was actually the big Englishman Graham, who had risen from his own bed on another sofa and was moving through the darkness toward the place from which his father's voice came . . .

Stockton's mind surged ahead, putting the pieces together and sensing what was about to happen. It horrified him so much he froze, unable to move or call out.

Pa's come looking for me again. . . . He's come in here 'cause he knows there ain't nobody living here no more . . . but he don't know that there are folks here tonight after all . . . bad folks . . . dangerous folks—

He heard the sound of struggle, a yell of fright from his father, a curse from Graham. A match flared, struck by Graham, and for a second Stockton saw light play across his father's face, looking startled and bewildered by the sight of Graham before him.

"*You* again!" Graham declared.

Josiah Stockton tried to speak, but his voice was cut off suddenly, and Stockton knew Graham had grabbed him by the throat.

A hundred past fantasies of seeing his cruel father die faded away for Stockton Shelley. This was his *father,* and a bad man was hurting him . . .

"What the hell's going on down there?" Evaline called from above.

Stockton leaped up and ran to Graham, whom he

began pounding and kicking as hard as he could. Graham swore but just kept on choking Josiah Shelley.

It registered with Graham that apparently this was the boy's father. But it did not matter. Graham had never been one to abide trouble with the same man twice, no matter what the circumstances. The second time was the last . . . every time.

"Let him go!" Stockton screamed, frantic, still fighting. "He's my pa! Let him go!"

Without even looking, Graham punched a fist backward and struck Stockton right on the mouth, knocking him down, making blood spurt from a cut lip.

Stockton was up again at once, fighting Graham once more. Then strong hands pulled him away— Brown, grabbing him from behind.

"He's killing my pa!" Stockton screamed. "Let me go!"

Brown dragged him backward across the room. Stockton watched in horror as Graham brought out a knife. As dark as the room was, Stockton could make out the shape of Graham's arm rising and the blade gripped in his fist. . . .

It swung down and Josiah Shelley gasped, then moaned. Then he made no more sound at all, and Stockton knew he was gone.

"No!" he screamed. "No, no, no, no. . . ."

Somehow he managed to pull free of Brown. He lunged toward Graham, fists flailing, feet kicking. . . .

Graham cursed and brought up his knife again, then swung it down once, twice. . . .

Bleeding and hurting, Stockton staggered away,

back into a dark hallway. There was the sound of a door opening and closing again.

"Hell, Graham, you stabbed the boy!" Brown exclaimed.

"He was annoying me," Graham replied, very calm. "But confound it all, go bring him back. I'll patch his wounds. I didn't cut him severely."

Swearing, Brown went into the hallway after Stockton.

"Graham, he ain't here."

"What?"

By now Evaline and Kevington were in the room, descended from above. "Where is he?" Kevington demanded.

"I heard a door," Brown said. "Wait. . . ."

He opened a door that seemingly led into a small storage room. But a strike of the match revealed another door on the other side, and blackness beyond it, and a staircase. . . .

"He said there were tunnels and passages all through this house," Kevington said. "The boy's escaping us! Go get him. . . . Bring him back!"

Evaline and Brown obeyed at once, descending the dark staircase swiftly, vanishing into blackness.

Graham did not move. "Let him go, I say," he muttered.

"Let him go? And alert the law to our presence here . . . and to the corpse you've now blessed us with? Why the hell did you kill that man?"

"Because he found us. And because he spilled beer on me on the street tonight."

Kevington swore bitterly. Graham simply sauntered away, through the dark, and lay down on his sofa again.

Brown and Evaline returned soon after.

"He's given us the slip," Evaline reported. "The little bastard must know five or six different ways in and out of this house."

"He may go to the law," Kevington said. "That's trouble and delay we do not need. Come on. Let's gather our goods and leave here."

"In the middle of the night?"

"That's right. We have no time for entanglements with the local constabulary. We're leaving this house tonight, and at first light we'll set out to find that ghost town on our own. There can't be many roads across that mountain . . . only one, if we're fortunate. We don't need that boy to track down Kenton and Victoria. We'll get by without him."

"What if we can't find that ghost town?"

"We'll find it. We'll find it if we have to search to the very edges of hell. Now, move with haste. We must leave this house before that little escapee brings back trouble to us. I have no desire to attempt to justify the killing of an intruder, especially considering that we are intruders here ourselves."

CHAPTER

30

AFTERNOON, TWO DAYS LATER

ROXANNE GUNNISON STOOD BESIDE THE BED, watching Rachel Frye sleep, and tried to remember if she'd ever seen anyone look so pale. She reached down and lightly touched Rachel's forehead, taking care not to disturb her. Rachel was fevered. Roxanne shook her head sadly and left the room.

She walked down the hall a few yards and entered the adjacent room, where Alex was seated by the window, cleaning his pistol and looking quite somber. Outside, beyond the window, the ragged and rugged farrago of Culvertown, Colorado, was visible. Roxanne hadn't liked Culvertown when she visited it recently, and she didn't like it now.

Yet she felt they were supposed to be here. She was not a superstitious woman by nature, but finding that sketched-upon envelope in the Buckeye Cafe just a short distance down this very street had certainly seemed like a stroke of destiny to her. If not for that event, none of this would be transpiring.

"She's worse, I think," Rachel said. "The strain of all this hard travel has been too much for someone who not all that long ago was lying senseless in a hospital bed."

"We shouldn't have brought her," Gunnison said, rubbing the gun barrel gently with a lightly oiled cloth.

"Perhaps not. But it seemed the only possible thing at the time."

They were in the Culvertown Hotel, on the second floor, in the very room, in fact, that Dr. David Kevington had occupied until he and the men with him had simply vanished without paying. But Gunnison knew none of this. They had come here, arriving late the prior evening, simply because they had needed rooms after a long and wearying railroad journey across a big part of the nation, with Rachel Frye growing more weak and sick with each mile.

Now Gunnison was not quite sure what to do. Rachel needed medical care, and he'd already learned from the locals about the violent deaths of Jack Livingston and an unidentified stranger up in the Livingston mansion.

KB FOUND IN CULVERTOWN. LIVINGSTON HOUSE. PLEASE COME.

So had read the telegram Billy Connery had flashed to New York. Well, Gunnison had come, but there was no access to the Livingston house, no Billy Connery, and so far no Kenton.

He was scared out of his wits that the unidentified stranger who had died with Jack Livingston might have been Kenton.

And where the devil was Billy Connery? And why hadn't he sent a more complete and informative telegram? Did Kenton have Victoria with him up in the Livingston house? If so, where was she now?

Too many questions, too few answers, and Gunnison was growing downright irritable about it.

"She's going to need a doctor," Roxanne said.

"I know," Gunnison snapped. "I'll fetch her one, as quickly as I can. Just let me finish cleaning this pistol. Do you mind?"

Roxanne stared at him silently a moment. "No. What I do mind is having my head taken off for a mere comment."

Gunnison softened. "I'm sorry. I'm just on edge . . . and scared. I have this feeling that something has happened to Kenton. Maybe to Billy, too."

"The dead men in the Livingston house?" Gunnison had already told his wife about that bit of grim local news.

"Yes. I'm afraid Kenton might have been one of them."

"Wouldn't he have been identified, though? His face is famous."

"Everyone believes Kenton has been dead for months. They'd just assume this dead man was one who resembled him."

"What are we going to do, Alex?"

Gunnison laid his work aside and stared out the window at the street. "Well, I suppose that we need to make sure Rachel is cared for. I need to find a physician."

"Yes. I think so. She has a fever right now."

Gunnison stood, went to Roxanne, and wrapped his arms around her. "I wish I could say I felt good about all this. But I don't. Since we've gotten here I've had the worst feeling about it all. But I'm glad you're here with me. It makes it better."

She kissed him. "If Kenton is alive, we'll find hiim. And Victoria, too."

"I'm going to go find a physician for Rachel," Gunnison said.

"You're a good man, Alex Gunnison."

"I don't know about that. But I do know I'm a very worried one."

On the far side of Culvertown, a man known to most as Preacher Joe Sammons walked up a rocky hillside toward a church house he had built three years ago almost entirely by himself. It was Friday, and Sammons's habit was to spend an hour or two each Friday getting the church cleaned up for the weekend, stocking the supply of firewood. He would also pray in the empty sanctuary for each of the members of his small congregation, who at the moment were scattered out across Culvertown and its vicinity. Sammons was a big, burly man, rough and leathery, carrying on his body the scars of what had once been a rowdy and violent life. Now he was known as the gentlest, kindest, most tender man in all Culvertown, and even those who declined to set foot in his church respected him.

He never locked the building, believing it should always be open for the sake of those who wished to pray. In Culvertown there were far too few of these, but Sammons was an optimist. Someday the fire of faith would sweep across these mountains, and he intended to be there to see it. Maybe he would even be the one to spark it, if God was kind enough to give him the privilege.

The interior of the church was shadowy and cool. Sammons walked through it, the heels of his boots clumping heavily on the wooden floor. He was proud of this little building, simple as it was. Its interior was spotlessly clean, thanks to his constant attention to it, and painted a clean, oily white.

Sammons went to a closet in the corner and pulled out a broom. He began to sweep between the pews, whistling softly to himself.

Within a couple of minutes he began to get an odd feeling. He stopped sweeping.

"Hello? Is there somebody here?"

He heard the faintest kind of noise in response. Just a whisper of sound, so low that Sammons couldn't tell what it was.

"Hello?" he said again as he began winding between the pews, looking for the source of the sound.

He found it near the front, in the person of young Stockton Shelley. Sammons knew Stockton well; he'd tried many times to bring the poor boy under his influence and lessen the influence of his hard-drinking, abusive father. Sammons worried about Stockton a lot and prayed for him daily.

Stockton was curled up like an unborn child, lying on the pew on his side, staring at the back of the pew before him. His eyes were wide open, hardly blinking, and he was moving very slightly, kind of a childish rocking. There was blood on him, crusted and rusty-colored.

"Stockton, son, what's happened to you?" Sammons said, kneeling between the pews and laying a hand gently on Stockton's shoulder. Stockton flinched at the touch, his eyes still fixed.

"Stockton, it's me: Preacher Joe. It's all right. . . . You can talk to me."

Stockton continued to stare, hardly seeming aware that Sammons was there.

Sammons moved, lowering his head so that his face came into the line of view of Stockton's staring eyes. He looked into the boy's face a few moments and noticed a subtle change. Stockton looked at him, and his lips began to tremble.

Sammons smiled and nodded. "That's right, Stockton. It's just me. I'll help you out, no matter what's wrong."

Stockton began to cry. His lips moved.

"What's that? I didn't hear."

"He's dead," Stockton whispered.

"Who?"

"My pa. He's dead."

Sammons developed a terrible suspicion. This boy, threatened and abused, had killed his own father! That might account for the blood.

"Let's sit you up and take a look at you, Stockton."

Stockton sat up. Sammons saw the cuts in his shirt that told him the dried blood was at least in part Stockton's own. Someone had knifed this boy.

"Did your pa do this to you?"

Stockton shook his head.

"How long have you been hiding here?"

"I don't remember."

"Come on, son. We're going to get you to Doc Asheman. He'll look you over and see what needs fixing, all right?"

Stockton did not reply but did stand. The poor boy was weak and deep in some sort of numbing shock, mind and body, and Sammons wondered what this boy had experienced, and seen, to make him be this way. The Stockton Shelley he had always known was cocksure and sarcastic, hiding fear and loneliness behind a mask of bravado . . . a far cry from the pitiful creature Sammons saw now.

Stockton made it out of the church and down the hill, then slumped to the ground, too weak to continue.

"Don't worry about it, Stockton," Sammons said. "I'll carry you to my house and hitch up the wagon. Then you can lie down and I'll take you in to Dr. Asheman."

CHAPTER

31

ROXANNE SAT ON THE EDGE OF RACHEL'S BED AND wondered how long it would take for her husband to locate a physician in this town. It seemed to her that Rachel's fever was mounting, and she looked worse by the hour.

Hurry, Alex.

Rachel opened her eyes. "I feel like I'm aflame," she said.

"I'll get something to cool you," Roxanne told her. "And Alex will be back soon, with a physician, I hope. He's out looking now."

"You're very kind to me."

"You're our friend, Rachel. It's our pleasure to be kind. Would you like me to bathe your brow with a damp cloth?"

"Yes, mum, if you don't mind."

"Of course I don't mind." Roxanne looked around for a cloth but could not find one. But she recalled that a handkerchief lay on the chest in her and Alex's room next door.

"I'll be right back," she said to Rachel, and went to get the handkerchief.

A minute later, she was seated on the bedside again, the cloth dampened by water from the basin. She dabbed it lightly on Rachel's hot brow.

"Thank you so much," Rachel said. "It's wonderfully cool."

Roxanne smiled and dipped the handkerchief in the basin again. As she did so, she noticed something she had not before.

"Well, that's a surprise," she said. "I didn't realize that Alex had monogrammed handkerchiefs . . . but wait a moment. These aren't Alex's initials."

On the corner of the white handkerchief were the embroidered and highly stylized initials *D. K.*

Rachel turned her head and looked at the handkerchief. "Oh . . . dear God. . . ."

"What is it?"

"The letters . . . they are the same as those on Dr. Kevington's house!"

"Dr. David Kevington? *That* Dr. Kevington?"

"Yes! The shape of the letters, the way they are . . . it's exactly the same! I grew up seeing those letters above the door of his house. . . . I know those letters. The handkerchief has to be his!"

"Rachel, it hardly seems likely. This handkerchief was on the chest of drawers in my room. I assumed it was one Alex had placed there."

"He is here, Roxanne. That is his handkerchief."

"Please, Rachel. Don't say that. You know there

are many people with those initials. If the style is the same, it's only coincidence."

"No . . . he's here. He's come here for the same reason we have, to find Brady Kenton and Victoria! He's here!"

Rachel was drifting toward hysteria . . . and Roxanne was beginning to wonder if she might be right. If Kevington had set an agent to following them all the way to New York, why should it be unlikely that he would come to this town if he, too, had found evidence that Kenton and Victoria were here?

"Rachel, please try not to worry. We don't really know why this handkerchief is here, or whose it is. Alex will be back soon. . . . We'll show it to him. Now, would you like me to bathe your brow some more?"

"Not with that cloth."

Roxanne forced out a smile. "Very well. I'll find another."

Gunnison learned the location of Dr. Asheman's office from a woman sweeping the porch of her cabin. He walked there with a broad and fast stride, not only because of his concern for Rachel but also because of the inexplicable sense of something being amiss.

He climbed the stairs to the office and knocked on the door. No answer. He looked through the window on the door but couldn't see anything through the curtain.

Glancing down, he saw that a little hand-lettered

placard had fallen from the window to his feet. BACK
IN FIFTEEN MINUTES.

Well, it would help to know whether the fifteen-
minute count started ten minutes ago or one. Either
way, he'd wait.

He tried opening the door and found it unlocked.
He pushed it open a foot and found himself looking
into an outer office, off of which two other doors
opened. One of them was ajar. "Hello?" he said, in
case the doctor was back in that room and hadn't
heard his first knock.

In reply he heard a faint groan. Probably a patient
back there.

"Doctor? Is that you?"

The groan was a little louder this time . . . and there
was something about it that caught his attention.

Gunnison paused, then said, "Are you all right?"

Not a groan this time, but a word, barely whispered
and very hoarse: "Alex?"

Gunnison was stunned. . . . Then he recognized the
voice.

He burst into the office and went straight to the
back room. "Billy?"

"Alex. . . ."

Sure enough, it was Billy Connery back there. He
was thin and weak and bandaged and trying to sit up.
His right hand lightly gripped a bandage around his
throat.

"Merciful heaven, Billy, what happened to you?"

"Throat . . . my throat was cut. . . ."

Gunnison gaped. "Your throat was cut. . . . Who? Why?"

"Can hardly . . . talk . . . couldn't talk . . . at all until . . . yesterday. . . ."

Gunnison scrambled about until he found a notepad and pencil. "Here, Billy . . . write it down. Take your time. . . . Don't try to talk."

Connery nodded. Gunnison helped him sit up, the exertion of that alone causing Billy to wince and become pale as the blood drained away from his head.

"Billy, tell me one thing: did you actually meet Kenton?"

Connery shook his head.

"But he was here?"

Connery whispered, "Yes. . . ."

"Don't say anything more. Just write."

Gunnison grabbed a chair and pulled it up to Connery's bedside. Forgotten now were Rachel's fever and his promise to Roxanne to hurry back with the doctor.

He sat squirming, as keyed up as a child awaiting a gift, as Billy Connery began to write.

CHAPTER

32

DR. DAVID KEVINGTON, TIRED, DIRTY, SUNBURNED, and angry, swore loudly and sat down on a boulder beside the trail. Or was it a trail or just a path made by the passing of wild game? He and his companions had crossed the mountain in the darkness and lost the road in the process, and now they'd wandered so far and lost themselves so thoroughly in the wilderness that it was easy to imagine that there never had been a human presence in this region at all.

"We're going to have to go back to Culvertown," Evaline said. "This ain't working. We're not going to find that ghost town . . . if there is any such damn place. I think we've been lied to."

"I'm hungrier than a redskin in winter," Brown said. "We've ate up every bit of food we brought, and the last stream I drank out of tasted like a buffalo had pissed in it. I say we go back. If there really is such a town as Caylee, we can find out how to get there and not just wander through all the backside of Pharaoh's Egypt to find it . . . or not find it."

Kevington looked at him bitterly. "I'll not turn back without finding Kenton."

"Begging your almighty pardon, sir, and with all due respect to you for the good wages you're paying us, it seems to me you'll be a damn sight more likely to find Kenton by going back than by going forward."

"And do you know the way back, Mr. Evaline?"

"I know where the mountaintop is. I know how to look for smoke plumes to tell me where the town is. The trouble with Caylee is that it's a ghost town, and you don't see smoke plumes from ghost towns."

"He's right, Dr. Kevington," Brown said. "If there's an abandoned town hereabouts, you'd think we'd find more trails. And if Kenton was holed up there, you'd think he'd build a fire every now and then. There'd be smoke. But there's been no smoke on this side of the mountain."

"We need to go back, sir," Evaline said. "We'll find Kenton a lot faster going back than going forward. If he's here to be found at all. He's had enough time he could have taken her a long distance. We've been looking out here for two days, sir."

"We've got to go back," Brown affirmed again.

"Go back?" Kevington said, chuckling. "So you think we would go back? Might I remind you what we left lying on the floor of that mansion? A dead body. Two days ago. That body surely has been found by now. And keep in mind that the boy got away. He fled, stabbed but alive, and fully able to talk. If we go back to Culvertown, we go back to face arrest."

Brown and Evaline stared at him, frowning, apparently having not thought of this before.

Kevington looked back at them with contempt. "You were supposed to be the best, the most clever, the most persistent, the most heartless when the situation called for it. But now I must wonder. If you are representative of the best that this nation offers, then I stand astounded that the colonies managed to ever win the war." He laughed coldly. "What do you think, Graham?"

"Actually, sir, I'm not thinking of much at all," Graham replied. He'd been sitting in silence on a log nearby, smoking his pipe. "I've been too busy watching that smoke rise yonder."

It took a moment for the significance to sink in. "Smoke?" Kevington stood and turned.

Miles away, a thin line of smoke rose toward the sky where none had been before.

Kevington smiled. "Gentlemen, I believe we just found the town of Caylee."

Kenton knelt by the fireplace, slowly turning the spit upon which he had speared three rabbits. The scent was mouthwateringly good. He'd snared the rabbits during the afternoon, desperate to provide himself and Victoria with meat.

The little bit of food they had brought with them out of Livingston's mansion was almost gone.

Kenton worried about the fire, though. He'd deliberately avoided building one as long as he and Victoria had been here . . . until now, when the necessities of cooking forced it. With any luck he would get the cooking quickly done and the fire out and no one would notice the plume.

In the absence of such evidence as smoke plumes, Kenton actually felt relatively safe here. With much searching and great exertion, he had finally managed to find the house that Jack had used for his illicit romantic dalliances. It was quite a feat of engineering, in its way: a house that looked run-down and barren from the outside but which was actually quite livable inside. It was funny, in its way, Jack having gone to this trouble just to keep his love affair secret. It reflected his eccentricity.

Now the place was protection for Kenton and Victoria. Kenton could only hope it was protection enough.

He was eager to leave here, but Victoria was tired, weak, not ready for travel. And where would they go? Anywhere they went, Kevington would follow.

For now Kenton refused to think further than the next hour or so. At the moment all that mattered was roasting these rabbits and feeding himself and his wife, who slept now on a bed in the other room of this two-room house. Then he would put out the fire and worry about the next hour when it came.

But at some point, this had to end. He would have to deal with Kevington in a final way. There would have to be a showdown.

But how, with Victoria to be protected? She was a woman strong of heart but not of body.

Kenton stared into the flames, watching the rabbits

roast, and prayed for guidance, for help, and for rescue.

And he prayed that if Kevington was out there somewhere, still looking, he would not find this house.

CHAPTER

33

THE FIFTEEN-MINUTE ABSENCE OF DR. ASHEMAN HAD stretched to nearly an hour by the time Billy Connery put down his pen and handed the pad to Alex Gunnison.

His work as an illustrator had given Connery the gift of a nimble pen. Despite his weak condition, he managed with succinctness and celerity to present Gunnison a written account of what had happened to him since his arrival at Culvertown. His account ended with his being stabbed and slashed by the man McCurden, who had initially presented himself to Connery as one Jim Grant.

Gunnison read the account quickly, then again more slowly. "So we really don't know what has become of Kenton," he said. "You never actually saw him yourself."

"No," Connery whispered.

At that point the outer door opened. Someone strode across the room and entered Connery's bedroom. It was a tall, tired-looking man, who was startled to see Gunnison there. He approached him with an outstretched hand and a serious look upon his face.

"My name is Asheman. This is my clinic. I gather you've talked to my patient."

"Yes. . . . I'm Gunnison, Alexander Gunnison. I work with your patient."

"I hope you haven't had him talking much. His throat was slashed and it's too early for him to be using his voice. He's lucky to have a voice at all."

"Yes. Don't worry. I've had him writing rather than speaking."

"How did you know he was here?"

"I didn't. Finding him was a surprise. I actually came looking for you, Doctor."

"You're ill?"

"No. But there is a woman at the hotel, Miss Rachel Frye, who is fevered and in need of your help."

Asheman sighed. It had been a long day already. "Very well. I'll go to her. But tell me, is she—"

The outer door of the office literally burst inward with a crash.

"Asheman! Doc, are you here?"

Asheman headed out the door. "I'm here, Preacher. What's—oh, my goodness."

Sammons carried in his arms the blood-crusted, weakened form of Stockton Shelley.

"The boy's been stabbed, Doc. But not just now. . . . I found him hiding in the church. He says he can't remember how long he's been there."

"Get him on the table there, and help me cut those clothes off him." Asheman turned to Gunnison, who had also come out into the outer office. "Sir, unless that fevered woman is in the most severe condition, I'm afraid I must make a priority of this case."

"Indeed, Doctor. Miss Frye can wait. Perhaps, given the situation you face, I should try to bring her here rather than you go there."

"If you please, sir, I'll go to her. I've got only two beds here, and young Stockton is about to occupy the second one."

Asheman turned his attention to Stockton; Gunnison turned to go back into the room where Connery was . . . but Connery had gotten up and had entered the front room, leaning against the wall to keep from falling.

Asheman noticed what was happening. "Connery! What the devil . . . Get back in that bed before you collapse!"

Connery staggered forward instead. He had heard it all from the back room but had to confirm with his own eyes that it was Stockton Shelley in the room. He went to the table where Stockton had been placed. Asheman continued to protest, but Connery did not even hear him.

Stockton looked up and saw Connery. A spark of life returned to what had been a lusterless gaze.

"It's you. . . . I know you."

"What happened, Stockton?" Connery's voice sounded horrible, hardly audible at all.

Asheman swore and might have physically pushed Connery away had he not been in such bad shape. "What the devil is going on here? My patients are fraternizing now? Get back in that bed before you tear your wounds open again, Connery!"

Connery turned to Gunnison. His words came out riding the crests of his weak gasps of air. "This boy . . . is the one . . . who told me where . . . to find Kenton."

"Quit trying to talk!" the doctor barked, only to be ignored yet again.

Gunnison came closer to the table. Connery had described his encounter with Stockton in the written account he'd given to Gunnison. "Do you know where Kenton is?" he asked Stockton.

"I must insist . . ." Asheworth began, only to be cut off by Stockton.

"He was in the mansion. . . . Now there are men in town who are chasing him. They hurt me. And they murdered my father." Some emotional dam broke inside Stockton, and he began to cry. "They murdered my father!"

Now even Asheman was drawn in. "Your father has been killed, Stockton?"

"Yes. . . . He's in the mansion. . . . They tried to murder me, too."

Stockton's wailed declarations would have sounded hard to believe except for the evidence of the wounds on his small and pale body.

"Where is Kenton now?" Gunnison asked Stockton.

"Who is Kenton?" the doctor asked, only to be ignored.

"In Caylee," Stockton replied. "I think he is in Caylee. The men chasing him were going to go there. . . . They were going to pay me to take them."

Asheman seized control again. "That's enough, all of you!" He barked an order to Gunnison: "Help Connery get back to his bed, and for God's sake don't let him open his own wounds!" He turned to Sammons. "You'd best go fetch the marshal. This boy is talking about a murder having occurred, and if he's right, I don't think it's even been detected yet."

Sammons nodded and headed for the door without a word.

The doctor looked at Gunnison. "You may as well make yourself useful. Get that fool back into bed before he kills himself, then come help me with my patient."

CHAPTER

34

BY THE TIME GUNNISON RETURNED TO THE HOTEL almost three hours after he had left, his wife was overwhelmed with worry.

"Thank God!" she said as she embraced him. "I was afraid that Kevington had gotten you. He was here . . . right in this hotel, in the very room we've rented. At least, Rachel is sure he was. We found a handkerchief with his monogram that had been left on the dresser."

Gunnison, so laden with news of his own, could hardly find room in his mental basket to accommodate yet another item. But he knew there was not an immediate need to worry about Kevington, because he knew where Kevington almost certainly was.

"Where's the doctor?" Roxanne asked, only just then noticing that Gunnison had returned alone.

"The doctor is very occupied with two patients he has bedded down in his clinic across town. How is Rachel?"

"Doing better on her own, I'm glad to say. She's

sleeping now, and her fever is down. But tell me why these two patients are so important that the doctor refused to come see a sick woman?"

"Don't judge him harshly. From a medical stand-point he made the right decision, I have no doubt, because these patients are quite injured. One of them is a little street boy named Stockton Shelley, who has—listen to this!—been in contact with Kevington himself. And he is reasonably sure he knows where Kevington has gone . . . and where Kenton is. The other patient is Billy Connery."

"Billy! Why is he being treated?"

"Because somebody—one of Kevington's hired agents—cut his throat. He was left for dead in an alley, but survived, thank God."

"Oh, mercy! He'll live?"

"Amazingly, yes. The doctor said he was fortunate to fall in the way he did. The cut in his throat, maybe not as deep as his attacker thought, was held closed by the angle of his head when he passed out in the alley. Someone found him and got him to the doctor, and he's slowly getting better."

"How did he manage to get into a row with one of Kevington's agents?"

"It's a long story, one built of this piece and that, most of which I've only just learned. Billy has pro-vided me what he knows and experienced, and the little Shelley boy has contributed what he knows—including his witnessing of the murder of his own father by an agent of Kevington."

"Murder! Oh, Alex! This grows worse by the moment."

"Yes. And it may grow worse yet. Kevington may have already found Kenton and Victoria. And he has three hired guns with him. . . . They wouldn't have stood a chance."

"I think I need to sit down."

"Do. Let's both sit down, and I'll tell you what I've learned. This is cobbled together from assorted pieces of information, like I said, and I'll try to order it for you as I go. Forgive me if I backtrack some; it makes it easier to give you the context of what has happened.

"We already know from Rachel how the English side of this affair fell out: Kenton enters the house, finds Victoria but is caught by Kevington and made a prisoner, but still he manages to sneak word out to Rachel that she should flee back to the United States. She does, but her ship goes down off the coast. She is injured and goes into an extended, anonymous hospitalization in New York, unconscious much of that time, and of course is unable for a long time to contact us. When at last she does, you have also returned from your trip to Colorado, and have stumbled across that sketch that makes us realize Kenton is hiding here in Culvertown.

"All right. So I send Billy Connery to Culvertown, and he manages to learn very quickly, mostly from this little Stockton Shelley character, that Kenton really is in Culvertown and hiding out in the mansion of Jack Livingston, who, if I recall, has family ties to

Victoria. Kenton never talked much about that, but I'm sure I'm right. Anyway, Billy doesn't realize that an agent of Kevington's had already been sent to look for clues in St. Louis among Kenton's professional and personal circles, and this agent, named McCurtin or McCurden or something such as that, learns that Billy has run off to Culvertown and figures out that he might be coming because of Kenton. So McCurden follows right on Billy's heels, apparently follows Billy around town in secret, and learns along with Billy that Kenton really is holed up in the Livingston house.

"McCurden intercepts Billy before he can get up to the mansion and leaves him for dead with his throat cut in an alley. My guess is McCurden had come up with the idea of capturing Victoria for himself and holding her hostage, making Kevington pay him high dollar to get her back. But something goes wrong, and McCurden gets himself killed up in the mansion, along with Jack Livingston. My guess is the pair killed each other. Kenton and Victoria disappear, knowing now that Kevington is very seriously pursuing them. They head across the mountain for an abandoned mining town called Caylee. We guess this, anyway, because they happened to be spotted by young Shelley, heading in that direction, and apparently Jack Livingston had a sort of secret second dwelling there, a place they might logically go to hide in.

"Apparently McCurden must have telegraphed Kevington that he'd found Kenton, because Kevington and a couple of agents show up in town and begin going around looking for McCurden and bringing up the name of Brady Kenton, too. Stockton Shelley learns about this and decides he'll go tell Kevington— for a price—where he can find Brady Kenton. Kevington agrees to hire the boy for a guide to get them to Caylee, which apparently is a hard place to find, and the whole gaggle of them sneak up and hide out in the Livingston house, which of course is empty at that point. Stockton told me that one of Kevington's men was sent to find out whether one of the two men killed in the mansion earlier was McCurden. The fellow comes back and says that it was.

"Later on, Stockton's father goes hunting for him, and one of the places he looks is the mansion, because he knows Stockton has hid there in the past. One of Kevington's agents kills the man, before Stockton's eyes. Stockton attacks him, gets knifed up himself, but manages to get away. He's hurt, weak, sick with grief over his father's murder, and he goes to hide in a church, where the preacher found him earlier today. The preacher hauled him to the doctor at the same time I was there, looking for help for Rachel. And of course I'd stumbled across Billy Connery there as well and was getting a lot of this information from him even as they were coming in. After the doctor finished patching up Stockton, I interviewed the boy . . . and that's how all the pieces came together."

"It's astonishing . . . but where is Kevington?"

"Gone. I suspect he and his agents decided to go find Caylee on their own, since they lost Stockton.

And they've had about two days to find the place . . . and Kenton."

She thought about that somberly. "Maybe Kenton and Victoria didn't go there after all. Maybe they just kept moving."

"We can only hope. But I'm going to Caylee to see, Roxanne. I have to know if Kenton and Victoria are there."

"But Kevington is out there. . . . You could be in danger! You mustn't go alone. . . . You have to take an officer of the law with you."

"That option has been explored. All this news was borne to the town marshal before I came here, and he was uninterested in anything except that there is another corpse up in the mansion. As for Kenton, the marshal believes what the rest of the world does: that he's dead. Besides, he said, Caylee isn't in his jurisdiction."

"But you can't go alone!"

"I won't. I'm taking a man with me. He knows where Caylee is, and he's a good man in a fight. Says that when he fights, God fights with him."

"Who is this man?"

"His name is Sammons. He's the preacher who found the boy hiding in his church. And he tells me that when he has to be, he can be mean as the devil for the sake of righteousness."

"Can you trust him? And can a preacher really be a fighter?"

"This one can, I believe. You'll know what I mean when you see him."

"Will he come here?"

"Yes. Before dawn tomorrow. He's bringing me a horse and saddle and rifle. At first light, he and I will ride out for Caylee."

Kenton opened his eyes and sat up in the bed, drawing in a gasp of air. He stared into the darkness, unsure what had awakened him.

Beside him, Victoria stirred a little but did not wake up. He looked at her, barely able to see her outline in the dark room, and said a quiet prayer of thanks that, since they had come to Caylee, she had allowed him to sleep in her bed.

Kenton remained quiet, unmoving, trying to figure out what had made him wake up. And he wondered, too, why he felt so afraid right now.

He'd spent a lifetime trusting his instincts, so he didn't dismiss the alarm sounding in his mind. He quietly slipped out of bed and crept to the door. He opened it and passed through.

He was not outside. Jack Livingston's clever interior construction involved what was essentially a house within a house, walls erected a few feet back from the actual exterior walls, creating a box that hid everything inside, including most light.

Kenton was outside that box now and moved carefully. He slipped toward the nearest window and looked out into the night. He saw nothing. He went to the other side of the house and looked out a window there.

Quickly he ducked again, his heart rising in his chest.

He crept back to the door to the inner part of the dwelling and reentered. He went to Victoria's side.

"Victoria, dear, wake up . . . quietly. They've come. They're here . . . and we must do nothing to alert them as to where we are."

It took a couple of moments for her to comprehend.

"David is here?"

"Yes. With others. And they're looking for us right now."

CHAPTER

35

SAMMONS WAS THERE EVEN EARLIER THAN PROMISED, bringing good horses, rifles, and the news that he'd just spent an hour praying for their mission. He was confident God would give them the victory . . . but he wasn't sure it would be a bloodless one.

"I can assure you it probably will not be, if we actually encounter Kevington," Gunnison said, out of earshot of his wife. "He will fight to the death before he'll let Kenton take away the woman he sees as his."

"She was a stolen woman, you said?" Sammons had been filled in by Gunnison the day before, but it had been a lot to absorb and he still didn't seem fully cognizant of it all.

"She was stolen, and hidden away in England for years, with Kenton believing she was dead."

"That's a great sin indeed. And this is a righteous battle."

"I can only hope it isn't a battle already completed. If Kevington found them . . ."

"Have faith, my friend. I believe we'll find them safe and sound."

"Why are you doing this?" Gunnison asked the preacher.

"Because I'm able to. I'm a good fighter, Mr. Gunnison. There was a time when I used that fighting skill in the wrong ways. I hurt people, hurt them bad. I've even killed men, sir. It was always what folks called 'fair fights,' but I can tell you that I'd have killed them all the same, fair fight or not. I regret all that. So now, I'm going to fight the good fight."

"Even for a stranger?"

"Brady Kenton a stranger? Everybody in the land knows and loves Brady Kenton."

Gunnison said good-bye to his wife and to Rachel, who without the help of a physician now seemed to be mending fast. They did not linger on their farewell or allow themselves to discuss the darker possibilities that lay ahead.

As Gunnison and Sammons rode out of town, Roxanne felt bitterly guilty for the thought that flashed without bidding through her mind: *If it is destined for Kevington to find Kenton and Victoria, I hope it's already happened. I want my husband to come back safe.*

She watched them ride away, their shadows stretching long in the light of the rising sun.

When the rising of the sun was a fading memory of an expired morning, Dr. David Kevington, exhausted, hungry, and frustrated, plopped down on the edge of a rotting boardwalk and shook his head. Graham was near, probably as hungry and perhaps as frustrated, but he seldom let his feelings show.

On down the street, Evaline and Brown were searching through empty buildings. They'd been complaining for the last hour, declaring that Kenton obviously was not in this town. Time to move on. The man had escaped and taken his woman with him, and Kevington would just have to accept it.

Kevington was not about to accept it. He would search this ghost town until every possible hiding place was ferreted out. If Brown and Evaline wished to be relieved of their duty, he'd be glad to oblige them with two quick shots to their heads. Right now it would be cathartic to do it.

Graham brought out his pipe and loaded it slowly. "Let me ask you something, Doc," he said. "Just to make sure I have my facts straight. You and Brady Kenton's wife were on a train together, and it crashed. Many years ago."

"I was on the same train. We were not together."

"Coincidence?"

"Not coincidence. I was following her."

"I see." He lit the pipe. "Following the wife of another man."

"She was his wife in the legal sense. But in the eyes of heaven she has always been my wife. She was meant for me."

"But she married another."

"She said words before a clergyman. I attach no significance to it."

"But Kenton obviously did. When he found out she was alive, he came all the way across the ocean to get her."

"What is your point, Graham?"

"I must say I admire Kenton for what he did. He showed a husband's true devotion, just as my father showed to my mother, may God rest them."

"A husband's true devotion, Mr. Graham, is what you see being carried out before your eyes at this moment. Do you think what Kenton did was remarkable? Look at what I've done! It was I who dared to claim the woman who was intended for me! It was I who saved her life and gave her a home, and love, and care, for so many years. Now I've followed her across an ocean again, and hired an army of men to find her and rescue her from her kidnapper."

"So it's Kenton who is the kidnapper."

Kevington studied Graham a few moments, then said, "This conversation will end. Now."

At that moment, three shots blasted from down the street, and they heard Brown scream in a remarkably high-pitched voice.

Kevington came to his feet and Graham knocked the ashes from his pipe. They picked up their rifles and trotted down the street in the direction from which the gunfire had come.

Unseen by them and at the far edge of Caylee, Alex Gunnison and Joe Sammons reined their tired horses to a halt and looked at each other.

"Gunfire, three shots," Gunnison said.

Two more shots rang out; it seemed they could hear a man screaming.

"Ride in or on foot?" Gunnison asked.

Sammons thought for a moment. "Ride into that barn there and leave the horses. On foot the rest of the way. We don't know what we're getting into."

CHAPTER

36

BRADY KENTON WAS TRYING HARD TO FEEL BAD FOR the man he'd just shot through the gut, but he just didn't have it in him. The man had been about to shoot him. It was a true case of self-defense.

More than that, it was defense of Victoria. She was hidden on the upper floor of what once had been a saloon. She and Kenton had slipped out of Jack Livingston's well-disguised house an hour ago, when Kevington and his searchers drew near and Kenton had been sure they were about to be detected.

Livingston had built himself a sort of trapdoor that opened onto a stone-floored area beneath the house upon which firewood was stored. The trapdoor, intended as a convenient way to bring wood in on cold days, had proved just as convenient as an escape route for a pursued man and woman.

Kenton had lodged Victoria in the upstairs of the former saloon, then had taken the role of the killdeer bird, allowing himself to be seen so that he could draw his pursuers away from where Victoria was hidden.

If Kevington got his hands on Victoria, it would be over. Kenton would be killed forthwith and Victoria hauled away, this time never to escape.

"Brown!" the second of the two gunmen yelled. "Brown, how bad you hit?"

"I'm gut-shot, Evaline! Help me, please . . ."

Kenton actually did feel sorry for the man now. He was writhing about in the dirt. He'd been emerging from an alley when he'd spotted Kenton trying to take cover behind a rusted piece of old mining equipment. Brown had prepared to take a shot at Kenton but had taken a slug through the gut instead. He was doomed. Wounds of this sort a man did not recover from.

With a new round levered into the chamber of the Winchester he'd taken from Jack Livingston's mansion, Kenton watched Brown slow in his writhing and go quiet and still. He felt an odd sensation. It had been many years since he had been forced to kill a man, and it was not a pleasant feeling, even though the man he'd killed would have gladly killed him.

Now Kenton turned his attention to the other man, the one named Evaline. He'd heard him but not seen him, and there were plenty of places about in which a man could hide. Evaline might be sneaking up on him right now, even taking a bead.

Kenton was too edgy to stay put, and he was still too close to the saloon where Victoria hid. He'd hurriedly instructed her to keep deathly quiet, no matter what happened to him. If he died, she was to remain hidden until Kevington and his men were gone, then make her way back across to Culvertown, being sure to avoid Kevington, and wire Alex Gunnison at the *Illustrated American*.

But Kenton didn't intend to die here. He would fight his way out of this, no matter what it took. He'd not spent more than two decades searching out his stolen wife only to have Kevington rob him of her again by killing him.

Kenton rose and scrambled toward an old woodshed that was overgrown with ivy. A shot fired, the bullet singing past him. He caught a glimpse of the powderburst from the corner of his left eye.

Kenton dropped, rolled behind the woodshed, then scrambled back up and fired off a quick shot at the place he'd seen the powderburst. He saw Evaline dodge back behind a tree.

No sign of Kevington and the other man with him. Good in one way, bad in another. What if they had found Victoria?

Evaline popped off another shot at Kenton. The corner of the shed shuddered and splinters blasted off in all directions, stinging Kenton's face.

Victoria huddled in the corner of the old saloon loft, wincing every time she heard a shot. She was terrified for Kenton and full of hatred for David Kevington. She vowed that if her husband died, she would personally see that Kevington died as well, no matter what it took to bring it about.

She heard another round of shots, then the sound of feet pounding up the street outside.

Victoria pulled herself into an even smaller, tighter human ball, wishing she could simply vanish, and take her husband with her.

She prayed hard . . . and then heard something that caused her to cease to breathe for several seconds straight.

Somebody was downstairs, just below. A thumping sound . . . feet on the stairs?

She had to look, and did. With great relief she saw that the thumping was simply a loose hanging board, swinging in a breeze.

Encouraged, she moved to a window and carefully looked out. The street below was empty . . . but then she saw movement.

Her breath failed her again. David Kevington was down there, along with a man she did not recognize. They were both armed and heading up the street to the place where Kenton was still fighting.

Victoria wanted to weep. Kenton was one man, fighting impossible odds.

All because of her.

Kenton had left her with a pistol, to defend herself in case she was found.

She looked out the window, watching Kevington advance, and the man with him. The gunfight up the street was continuing . . . and now she saw even more men, two more, moving in on foot through an alley, coming from the other side of town.

How many men had Kevington brought? How

could Kenton be expected to single-handedly fight away four, five men?

Victoria said another fast prayer, checked her pistol, and turned to descend the stairs.

Kenton was lifting the rifle to fire at Evaline when he got a shot off first. The bullet struck Kenton's rifle in the stock, shattering it and inflicting a cut on his jaw. The rifle shivered out of Kenton's hands and fell, useless, to the ground.

Evaline laughed and emerged, coming in for the kill.

Kenton drew his pistol, stepped out, crouched, aimed, and shot Evaline through the forehead, two fast shots.

Even as Evaline fell dead, another shot blasted from up the street. Kenton's leg kicked out from beneath him, and he fell with a grunt. It was as if someone had just driven a hot metal stake through his calf.

Kenton saw him then: David Kevington, rifle in hand, coming toward him. Beside him was another man, also armed, this rifle smoking. Kenton knew who had shot him.

He lifted his pistol and fired at the man, narrowly missing him. A second shot did better.

Graham let out a yell as Kenton's bullet passed through his middle. He looked down, watching blood gout from the bullet hole, and shook his head. "I think you're on your own now, Doctor," he said to Kevington, and then pitched down on his face.

Kevington, seeing Kenton raising his pistol again,

headed for the nearest alley. Kenton fired at him, once, twice, missing both times.

The next click of the trigger fell on an empty cylinder. Kevington heard it and stopped in his tracks. He turned, facing Kenton, and laughed. "Well, my old nemesis!" he said. "It seems that the worm has suddenly turned!" Kevington advanced toward Kenton, working the lever of his rifle. "Where should I put the first bullet, my friend? Your leg? Your shoulder? Your gut?"

Kevington came right up to Kenton, who was about to make it onto his feet again. At the last moment, though, Kevington kicked Kenton's injured leg and made him fall again.

Kevington leaned over and glared down at the man he hated above all others. "I should have dealt with you in England when I had the chance. Too merciful, that's my problem. It always has been. Well, Kenton . . . it's time to say good-bye. I don't know where you've stashed Victoria, but I'll find her. For now, seeing you die is enough."

Kevington aimed his rifle at Kenton's forehead, squinting down the barrel.

Kenton shoved the rifle to the side just as it fired and wrenched it away, so hard he took some of the hide off Kevington's fingers. Kevington roared in anger and tried to grab the rifle again, but Kenton pounded him back with it, then flipped the rifle in the air. He levered it. . . .

Before Kenton could fire, Victoria did. Her bullet caught Kevington between the shoulder blades. He grunted loudly, turned, and sank to his knees.

"Victoria . . . dear God, Victoria . . ." He gaped at her, unable to believe the woman he had come this far to find had just shot him.

Victoria, trembling now, dropped the pistol. Kevington stared at it, then reached into his pocket and pulled out a small hideout gun. He lifted it, aimed it at Victoria . . .

From a kneeling posture, Preacher Joe Sammons fired three shots in succession, each of them striking in the area of David Kevington's heart.

Kevington fell straight back, dead well before his head bounced on the earth. Victoria fainted, and Kenton managed to rise.

Sammons stood slowly, bowed his head, and prayed for the soul of the man he had just killed.

Alex Gunnison was running up the street toward Kenton. "Kenton!" he shouted. "Kenton!" There was no need to say anything else.

Kenton's calf was bleeding, but he managed to stand upon it, even stagger forward. He was headed for Victoria.

Gunnison met him, threw his arms around him.

"Alex, where did you come from?"

"It's a long story . . . but there will be plenty of time to tell it. Thank God you're all right. Thank God!"

Kenton sat on the ground beside Victoria, who was reviving. She looked at him. "It's over?"

"Yes," he said. "It's over."

She smiled.

Gunnison touched Kenton on the shoulder and smiled at him and Victoria. "Come on," he said. "It's time for us all to go home."